There Are Not So Many Stars

definitive edition of *Pisot*

Isaí Moreno

I0682887

Translated by Arthur M. Dixon

Isaí Moreno

Translated by Arthur M. Dixon

There Are Not So Many Stars

definitive edition of *Pisot*

katakana
editores

There Are Not So Many Stars
Definitive Edition of *Pisot*
First Edition 2020

© Isaí Moreno

© Translated by Arthur M. Dixon

Cover image: Dígitos, Tiempo, Medición by Piro4D PIXABAY

© Published by katakana editores 2020

Editor: Omar Villasana
Design: Elisa Orozco
© Interior Images: Blanca Beatriz Caraballo

ISBN: 978-1-7341850-1-0

KATAKANA EDITORES CORP.
Weston FL 33331
✉ katakanaeditores@gmail.com

D uring the last years of the viceroyalty, in that New Spain that our novelists tend to ignore with a singular optimism—perhaps convinced that only in the matter of the present is it possible to reinvent a kinder fate—Isaí Moreno has given life to a strange literary figure. A wanderer through a circular, almost infinite tale, his character is called Policarpo de Salazar and he is a living logarithm, an obsessed calculist, a mathematician able to turn the visible into an operation of the unthinkable and to transform any urbane routine into dividend, divisor, quotient, and remainder, all with a single stroke of his voice.

As the focal point of the scientific gazes that fed the curiosities of our last colonial period—an age about to cross the threshold of revolution—Policarpo personifies the dynamics of a world that coexists in silence with a sensation of latent progress. This sense of imminent modernity is underpinned, in these pages, by the construction of the Palace of Mines by Manuel Tolsá, in the public streetlights that took their places on the streets of Mexico in those years, in the mechanics of the ringing bells of public buildings, in the accurate prediction of an eclipse that welcomes the reader to *There Are Not So Many Stars*, even in the everyday nature of voyages of circumnavigation around the Spanish world, and, above all, in the culture of education and instruction displayed by the book's learned men—many of whom are presented with great economy through Jesuit imagery. Nothing here is at a standstill, as we are informed by the experience of the clock—the reality that turned all times into determined instants and determining moments in the West—which runs through the book almost from its first pages.

To boldly complete this historical portrait of the viceroyalty, the relationship between magic and technology also claims a place of privilege here. What's more, the use of fantastic inventions breathes new life into an old mental schema better suited to worlds anchored in ambivalence because—it must be said—the providential explanation of human fate is dominant here alongside the great discourses of rationalist thought. In consequence, reading *There Are Not So Many Stars* represents, among so many things, a discovery of the broadsides suffered by the religious gaze when it perceived the change in sign of its most material exteriority. As a matter of fact, this obscurantism before the scientific consciousness represents the best possible narrative brew in which Policarpo might continue to intrigue us with the figures of his quests and the accounts of his killings.

Indeed, this mind whose extraordinary arithmetical skills tinge the enlightened air of the eighteenth century also transcends the condition of serial killer, of fugitive from justice, of great enemy of life and social peace. The numerical science that organizes his criminal existence will soon serve as a counterweight to help us understand the dynamics of historical reality that frame a great deal of the novel: the dawn of Independence. In fact, only in the *con-fusion* of such disparate events—a mathematics of homicide—will we come to understand that when a society insists on explaining itself solely as the daughter of its most lucid calculists, it must somehow inspire the creation of characters who, like Policarpo de Salazar, convoke in their des-

tinies the rejected ancestors of a past that, thanks to the literature of Isaí Moreno, today becomes truly ours.

In other words, who could doubt that the sickness of a past
age would be humanized not through the clinical analysis of its
forgotten homicides, not even through the justice passed down
by those who sought to correct its faults, but rather through the
cruelty of its murderers *made literature*? As Marc Bloch illus-
trates in his *Apology for History*, when the sciences that study
the past become rigid in their valuation of passions, literature
will ever come to their rescue, as a marvellous and innocuous
laboratory in which to test the imprudence of other assump-
tions—of other phobias, of other labors, of other masks?—and to
explain with greater humanity the avatars of a past that contin-
ues in our present. If *There Are Not So Many Stars* had no other virtue than that of recovering the antiheroes of our history, above
all those who lived alongside the roots of our scientific spirit,
this virtue would still justify its presence among the readers
of the twenty-first century: readers who, not to force the irony,
are often new Policarpos, especially when we recognize their
condition as blind manipulators of binary codes, as wayward
addicts to the immediacy of the numeric, or, why not, as con-
sciences trapped in the empty duplicities now displayed by the
verb *to navigate*.

Dividing his book into two novelesque periods, each very different from the other, Isaí Moreno also knows how to masterfully
evoke the complexity of mathematical discourse, its incomprehensible lexica, its overwhelming theorems, the most arid conjectures yet known to man... But it is not our ignorance that gives
strength to his explanations; it is the fact that the novel does not
seek to explain any of what it places within our reach. Through
this strategy, the book decides to return to our present in order
to narrate the quests of another character whom we somehow

sense as an extension of that ancestral murderer. Marino, the possible alter ego of Policarpo, lives among us, he is existing here and now, and he feeds off our modernity while he sets off in pursuit of something we can never quite define; it is neither a secret number nor an unknown formula, but rather, perhaps, an equation worthy of his intelligence, an algorithm that will give him the right to know he is superior, or, on the contrary, to declare himself insufficient and thereby take ownership of his death. In the end, this other historical frame, played in the key of a detective story, will lead us to conclude that numbers are not diabolical due to the obsessions they mediate, but rather due to the fear of proving that life can sometimes become a sequence, a chain, the frivolity of a calculation, or, even worse, pure ordered reason.

Numerical realities must not become tools of the future, nor convert our humanity into a religion of the mind, this novel tells us in a sly whisper while its chronological plasticity calls us, here with full force, to escape from the eruditions that seek to reduce our being in the world—the *Dasein* with which Heidegger sought to define our explanations of reality—to a pure numerical adjective. If mathematics are merely life transformed into signs, they must be lived and explained just like many other things deemed significant in our everyday existence must be lived and explained: the cure for an illness, the chemistry of flavors, the cartography of a continent, or the best use of rainwater in the most propitious season of the year, to cite a few examples.

At any rate... May God save us from a long prologue, said Quevedo upon concluding an introduction many pages long. It is better not to fall into contradictions, and simply to warn readers that they are about to walk through the streets of a tale that belongs to us, as it gives name to a part of our past with voices and instincts that inform much of what we are today. And while it is true that the murderers and the victims of *There Are Not So Many Stars* exhale the bitterness of numerical nonsense, we must be thankful for the fact that, although we may not understand many of its equations, this tale allows the lives we will never let die and the equations we will never solve to take on a certain clarity in the desire to reach the endpoint, the result of the plot, the product of a story that is unique and complex and fascinating and, above all, entertaining. ⊞

Javier Vargas de Luna

For Evelyn

FIRST ANALEPSIS
The Illusion

A devil taught me proportions and numbers and I built, with my eyes closed, a gallows, from which hangs a rope.

MARGUERITE YOURCENAR

On the 13th of May of 1752, in the old city of Mexico, an unusual incident occurred, an incident particularly grotesque. That day, a solar eclipse was expected, foreseen with precision by the astronomers of the day. Eclipses have always been objects of suspicion. For a year, learned men argued and refuted the assertions of other knowledgeable parties regarding these happenings that bring gloom and darken the hearts of men. On this subject, Don José Mariano de Medina, the eminent astronomer of the city of Puebla, wrote:

> I am certain that the havoc often wrought in such years is the child, not of the malign influences of the stars, but of the frights and terrors with which the dire predictions of the Astrologers afflict the apprehensive.

These words made the rounds in a little pamphlet (*Banishment of frights and terrors, vainly apprehended in the future quasi-total eclipse of the year 1752*), which became the object of great controversy and the target of many attacks, particularly from the physicist Narciso Marcop y Hecafoc, who published in turn a pamphlet-letter that he titled:. *Letter to a lady regarding the future eclipse of the 13th day of May of the present year of 1752 and regarding the printed letter written by the Hon. D. Joseph Mariano Medina*. In this text, the author redeemed the rights of fate in favor of ill-starred eclipses and *refuted* the enlightened rationalism of the foolish Medina. And so, among heated arguments and scholarly debates, warnings of calamity from the clerics, and the lamentations of the ignorant, the foretold eclipse came.

More than a few saw fit to commend their souls to Providence. When darkness began to fall, numerous old women came together in groups and lent their voices to litanies in a sad attempt to drive off the Evil One and his ill-fated souls. In the streets, the dogs howled, increasing with their cries the certainty of human misery, covered by the veil of that sinister night that menaced mankind. So believed those who stood alongside Don Juan de Salazar, creole silversmith and honorable old man, in his last moments, as he died a victim of the ravages of asthma. Nothing could be so cruel, they lamented, as witnessing a slow death, too weak-willed to cut life short with a single stroke. The old man's last labored breaths were reminiscent of those of a decrepit dog fading toward death in a corner, whose breath escapes in disjointed, sluggish shudders. The drama was accented further for those who knew that the old man was locked in a battle against death at the very moment of the eclipse, when men were at the mercy of forces that scourge their fates like a storm. The old man's gasps, which sometimes seemed to finally go out and put an end to his pain, restarted suddenly like a desperate whisper, determined to gulp a few more instants of even greater suffering into his throat, contorted by spasms. As the eclipse ended, the old man finally gave in to the dream of eternity. Friends and family cried. Even when the sun was shining once again, few took notice of its tremulous, weak appearance, like that of the mortuary candles that were lit for the dead man's wake. The grueling trip was ending… It was then that the mourners, amazed, heard the voice of an infant child who said: I know how many times he gasped before he died. Silence fell, and all turned to see who had spoken.

Their looks of surprise turned to expressions of horror when Policarpo uttered a number. He had counted the sick man's breaths throughout his unbearable agony, one by one until the end! The women stammered, trying to recite forgotten prayers. A freezing gust flooded the space, shooting through the bones of all those present. What sort of monstrosity was among them? Only demonic entities were capable of such aberrations. The boy was sick, perhaps possessed. That was it. Or perhaps the whole thing should be attributed to the eclipse. All of their minds retained the scene for future nightmares, they could not escape it for the rest of their days. Their innards shuddered as they watched the young boy of decidedly fair complexion turn with strange indifference and walk toward the patio of the house.

Yes, of course what had happened was the sign of a nearby, imminent calamity.

THE YEARS PASSED AND MANY OF DE SALAZAR'S NEIGHBORS who had awaited such a calamity died of old age. The grains of sand fell impassible through the hourglass at the pace of the halting breath of whomever persisted in remembering the event.

One cold afternoon in 1779, a certain old, toothless trollop ran through the streets, screaming. Her voice froze the blood: *The sickness, the sickness!* The people's distress owed not only to the news, but also to the looks of the woman who howled madly. Moments later, a cart ran her over and killed her in an instant. The cry of smallpox spread throughout the city, putting all its people on guard. It was too late. Thousands of citizens started to die. There were not enough carts to transport the bodies: some overturned on their hurried journeys, leaving the corpses uncovered. Those who were not carried to the cemetery were thrown into the canals or burned in the plazas. The infection flooded the deserted streets. As did the tears. In the center of the city, the church bells seconded the knell of the Old Bell of the Cathedral. The death's-head showed her rotten teeth, the cavities of her eyes shone with the yellow light of the candles: the despot laughed. Some succeeded in leaving the city uninfected, but reports told of the survivors being attacked by highwaymen on the roads, their wives raped and, in some cases, cut to pieces before them.

Weeks after the sickness Policarpo de Salazar reappeared walking down the avenues: that silhouette of yesteryear, now incarnated in a man of medium complexion, muscular body, and distrusting expression.

After the matter of the eclipse, aware that none desired to see him, he was sent by his parents to Puebla, the learned city of Palafox, where he was received by the benevolent and well instructed Jesuit José de Zaragoza. The priest educated him, bestowing his attention upon the youth with no care for what opinion the common folk might have of the anomalous Policarpo. The latter grew up there into a young man. Then he stayed there for another lustrum, living in the rooms of the Jesuit until his master departed on a missionary retreat that would end in the city of Valladolid. After rejecting the invitation proffered by José de Zaragoza to join him on this pious journey, Policarpo decided to learn of the world on his own account, beginning a tour of discoveries through the central and western parts of the country. For two more years, he wandered through settlements and villages before returning to the city of Mexico. No one remembered him when they saw him. When he learned of the deaths of the Salazar family (none survived smallpox), he was untroubled. He walked off in silence, and in a few days he established himself in an attic, gloomy but comfortable, whose walls kept out the din of carts and vendors of trinkets on the Street of Good Death.

HERNÁN CUEVAS WALKED HASTILY, ANXIOUSLY TO THE residence of Antonio de León y Gama. Hernán, a placid mestizo with graying hair, had spent fifteen years in the service of one of the greatest mathematicians in the country. Don Antonio was well known for his harsh critiques of the scientific publications of the *Gazette* (years later, in this medium, he would elegantly refute an anonymous man's demonstration of *squaring the circle*). He had elaborated the *Orthographic description* of a solar eclipse in 1778, along with interesting observations on the *Perpetual kalendar* of Fray Alejo García and the *Astronomic and harmonious hand* of Buenaventura de Ossorio, a work in which the latter described methods of finding the golden number and of calculating the epact, the solar *cicle*, the indiction, and the calends. Even the scholars of the Royal and Pontifical University sought his counsel, and he was also contacted by the mathematician José de Peredo, who presented him, not without enthusiasm, with his *Geometric demonstrations of the existence of God and on the Immortality of the Soul.* He was a friend of the Jesuit Francisco Javier Alegre, who wrote a dense treatise on gnomonics and another on elements of geometry. From the latter volume, he learned the construction and use of mathematical instruments in the manner of 's Gravesande, and he was imbued with pride in the science of New Spain, which was becoming independent of European minds.

De León y Gama loved Archimedes, he owned an edition translated from Greek to Latin of his *Arenario*, the sand reckoner, which he preferred to call the *Harenaria*, as well as another of the *Progymnasmata* of Tycho Brahe, Kepler's master, and one of *De umbris idearum* by the Italian heretic Bruno. When he was young, his grandmother had put before him the quote from Saint Augustine that reads:

The good Christian should beware of mathematicians and of all those who make vain prophecies. The danger already exists because the mathematicians have made a covenant with the devil to darken the spirit and confine man in the bonds of Hell.

In spite of this warning, he took the paths of the mathematician and the upright Christian at once: he was well aware of the matters of his time, and although he read Giordano Bruno and occasionally diverted himself with wagers and games of chance, he was considered a paragon of sobriety.

When the servant crossed the threshold into the house of De León y Gama, the latter had been anxiously awaiting him for some time. Have you seen him?, he asked impatiently. I have seen him, Don Antonio, answered Hernán. The learned man contemplated the dejected countenance of Cuevas. He did not seem himself, but the master knew the unpredictable character of the servant. Hernán, pressed De León y Gama, unable to contain his agitation, have you received him? Tell me what the man has told you. The other answered: He knows you, señor, he has heard of you and of your work, he also says he is willing to see it ... in a matter of days. A matter of days? Perhaps he is unwilling to engage in a simple exchange of words?, the mathematician snapped. It must be so, Don Antonio ... it must be so, said the old man before falling silent.

The room grew dark as evening fell, and a weak ray of sunlight faded away over the shelf on which books rested, covered in dust, many unopened since distant times. The scientist's eyes rested on them for a moment. So be it, instructed Antonio de León y Gama, I am in no hurry to see him, now go in peace, Don Hernán, in time I will send the man a letter. As Hernán walked away, the mathematician could see how his steps wavered. He whispered:

. . . I should like to say something, señor . . . the fact of the matter is . . . Have out with it then, you shall kill me with your mysteries, Don Hernán, the scientist lashed out, slamming shut the book through whose pages he leafed. I have no faith in him, whimpered Hernán, when I spoke with him it seemed I was addressing a dead man, and I liked it not at all. Mmmh, they say he is a strange individual. Yes, señor, said the old man, but the look of him . . ., to see his eyes is enough to make the skin crawl, and besides his voice is muffled, as if he suffered tonsillitis, and he is surrounded by strange things: on one of his walls hung the *Polyptych of Death*, or so I thought, and on the floor I saw a vessel of leeches. You know the *Polyptych of Death*, Hernán? Yes, Don Antonio, the servant confirmed, to his employer's surprise. De León y Gama declared: You must be ill, Hernán, remember that many physicians use leeches to bleed the sick and cure their wounds! If you say so, so be it, but there was something more that gave me fright, squeaked the servant's voice: upon his table sat a clock that turned backwards, the hands moved in reverse!

Antonio de León cast his eyes over his servant. He seemed to contemplate what he ought to say to the old man. On the bookshelf, he rummaged through sheaves of paper. He pulled out books. He blew the dust off documents until carefully removing a marked page.

I am accustomed to the strangeness of people, he said, those who dedicate themselves to science are not foreign to eccentricity. He held out the paper to his interlocutor. They sent this to me four years ago that I might revise it, I am no longer surprised by such things, and take note that it is a strange thing: it was written by a Franciscan of the province of Yucatán whom the Inquisition was on the point of hanging. Cuevas took the page and softly read aloud its title, as lengthy as baroque style dictates: *Lunar syzygies and squarings adjusted to the meridian of Mérida de Yucatán by a man of Antíctona or an inhabitant of the moon, and directed to the scholar Don Ambrosio de Echeverría, singer of funeral Kyries in the parish of Jesus of said city, presently professor of logarithmics in the town of Mama of the peninsula of Yucatán, in the year of our Lord 1775.*

My Lord, Don Hernán!, the wise man exclaimed, a scholarly friar speaking of inhabitants of the moon. God save us!, the good servant crossed himself as he answered. The man had had enough for that day, he left that place to complete his other important duties. De León y Gama remained with his books in silence. He thought of the individual they had discussed. He truly was strange. But it was rumored that he had a rare skill for counting great numbers of objects and for mental calculations. That had kept him up at night. After a grueling day, he deemed it worthwhile to continue reading a little longer. He lit his oil lamp, whose light illuminated the room just as it projected a host of shadows that danced to the rhythm of the flame.

THE DEVICE TURNED, OBEYING THE IMMUTABLE LAWS OF synchrony. Every piece communicated a precise movement to every other piece through the rigorous metal of its structure. The tension of a spring was released soundly through every tooth of the gears until flowing into an element that tirelessly oscillated around itself, from the center of its center, to lay down the rules that govern the matters of men.

The clockmaker's hands adjusted the artefact like a deity at the moment of putting the finishing touches on the creation that would be, by design, the proof of the *mysterium* for all future to come. It was an English clock, an impeccable instrument whose screws and gears were assembled in person by Ramsden himself, a man impassioned by exactitude and expertise. A belonging of a wealthy cacao merchant from Conception Street. The *tick-tock* produced an echo that ricocheted off the walls of the locked room, scarcely illuminated by two dying candles. And so, while the clock-maker watched the restless oscillation of the bronze balance wheel, the labyrinths of his memory twisted in malicious ways and led to the days when he would learn clockmaking and the terrible art of the *universal klock*, the technique with which to adjust the machine's synchrony to that of the heavenly bodies. His master would say: *time and fate are one and the same.*

Mastery of this art required years of training in the variation of times and seasons, the observation of stars, and the falling of the grains of sand in the hourglass. Also necessary was a serene consciousness of death, the guiding engine of the cogs' movement, as well as ample skill in the manipulation of numbers. Numbers were his first vocation. He counted from an early age. Numbers and more numbers were pronounced by his mouth. No one ever discovered the origin of this fondness. He counted everything in his sight: the birds in the poplar trees, the cirrus clouds in the sky, the balconies over the plazas, the houses on the streets, the streets themselves. He enumerated the peals of the church bells, the steps of a passerby from one place to another, the words in the Sunday sermon, the letters of one book or another… Once he wanted to count the lights of the starry sky, but sleep overcame him before he could succeed, and he plunged down a dark precipice where the confounded soul discovers new preferences. From then on, he experienced a singular pleasure only when counting exceptional things, like the caws of the crows, the twitters of an owl foreseeing death, the moans before the orgasms of the maids as they copulated in the granary with the servants, the pitiful howls of the dogs left outside or the tolls of the bells on funeral days. His tutor, José de Zaragoza, was unsettled to find him counting the ants that devoured the cadaver of a bird.

One day, by chance, he discovered his ability to make calculations without using paper: he returned to De Zaragoza's house and, after having numbered the houses on a certain avenue by sight, he unwittingly pronounced a figure. He took little time to realize that the number was none other than the sum of those he had observed, a fact he confirmed by scratching out the sum on the floor with a piece of coal. All *appeared* in his mind. In time, he was able to know if the household accounts were exact with a single glance, and often he would calculate even the longest arithmetic in a matter of seconds. Don Miguel Francisco de Ilarregui, the astronomer of Puebla, requested that he compute the epacts of the lunar year. On another occasion, on a visit with his guardian to the Palafox library, he mentally raised the quantity of books on its shelves to the second power and then to the third, leaving all those present open-mouthed. Numbers were the reason of his existence.

When José de Zaragoza departed on a long mission of evangelization, he commended his student to God and wished him luck in the trade for which he was instructed. He could do as he wished. The student proceeded to mourn for three days. After this, he felt himself to be his own master, and he decided to test his fortune elsewhere. He passed through the settlements of Cholula, Huejotzingo, and the Valley of Texmelucan. He did dealings with thieves and paupers. He lived with heretics and swindlers of all stripes. He slept alongside adventurers and rebels who already spoke of freeing the masses from the Spanish crown. By day he worked for farmers and landholders and by night he sought shelter in nearby inns. On one occasion, in the fine old lodging *El Fogón*, he awoke with a start: sticky drops of sweat wetted his forehead. He felt the *urgency* of something. A dream brought to his memory that past instant that changed his life and caused his exile. The day of the eclipse. A stinging larva began to wind its way through the interstices of his gut. He crossed himself several times, as he had learned from De Zaragoza, but Providence refused to come to his aid. After several months, he understood that he could no longer contain himself. In the inns, he frequented the prostitutes who softly called him to their quarters: most of the women were toothless and ugly, only a few were young like Policarpo. One of them, Crescencia, took it upon herself to instruct him in the pleasures of the flesh, which at first drew out delight from Policarpo, and then a deep regret due to the prior teachings of his mentor. The Jesuit had warned him of the injurious temptation of women of all classes. In the night, Crescencia slept beside Policarpo, but he touched her no more. He thought again of his *essential* need, impossible to decipher. He made himself present around the gravely ill, but none was close enough to death. He looked to places where the work was dangerous, but there were no accidents to claim lives, just as there were no victims of knife thrusts or fatal blows to be found when he walked the paths frequented by highwaymen. Once again, he lay awake throughout the night, sunken in seas of unease, while the young prostitute pressed her body against his, pronouncing in her sleep the names of former lovers. Policarpo gave the woman the few coins he had left and requested that she leave forever. He allowed a few weeks to pass until, a certain Sunday, late in the afternoon and taking advantage of a shepherd's inattention, he snatched up a little lamb. He brought the creature to his inn. When night fell, under the cover of the darkness whose dominions cover half the world, he strangled the animal with measured pressure such that he might plainly hear and enumerate the signs of its asfixia. He was scarcely soothed. Not long later, he strangled again, this time a dog. More sheep followed. When no such animals were to be found, he had to settle for hens. Sometimes he found a way into the stables at night and with a rope he strangled mules and mares. The people began to grow alarmed upon discovering their dead beasts, they formed groups that patrolled the paths with torches and lamps at night, preceded by sharp-nosed dogs. He fled to other villages and took refuge in the deep forests of Popocatépetl. Near an abandoned shack, he found a huge goose and carried it away. As he began his ritual of death with the bird, the animal forcefully flapped its wings and managed to free its neck for a moment, giving him a strong blow with its beak, straight to the throat: from then on, the timbre of his voice was diminished. This characteristic, along with his paleness and the lost look in his eyes, gave him the appearance of a talking automaton.

Only after fifteen months could De Salazar feel complete relief: he was walking along a stream when he reached the spot where a peasant was bathing. He hid himself among the bushes of the hollow adjacent to the river so as not to be seen and waited coldly for the man to dress himself. Suddenly, like an abrupt gust of wind, he fell upon him and tightened his grip around the neck of his prey. By then, his hands were already two iron tongs that squeezed shut with purpose, with controlled doses of pressure, like a medieval mechanism constructed for this very aim. The peasant, with panicked eyes, gasped on his knees before his executioner, who gasped aloud as well, but with pleasure, until all was reduced to a number. In the end, satisfied, on the trunk of the tree nearest the cadaver, he carved the crucial figure. It was a beautiful number, odd and prime.

After long dalliances, he decided to return to the place that saw him born. He arrived at midday with a battered case that contained his scarce belongings. He advanced through streets that he had not seen in many years, but that he recognized in spite of their changes. Policarpo de Salazar y Hurtado was now learned in the matters of life and he boasted three occupations: he was clockmaker, calculist, and murderer.

THE THREE MEN CAME TOGETHER IN THE MATHEMATICIAN'S study. De León y Gama had made three attempts to meet with Policarpo: the latter finally accepted after becoming aware of the scientist's reputation and their common interest in figures and the measurement of time. Not even the lit candle could dissipate the fog that seemed to emanate from the calculist's eyes, which glistened at intervals like those of a reptile about to sink in its fangs and drive home its poison. On the table lay several open books, among them one by Gamarra y Dávalos with abbreviated calculations of enormous numerals, and *The Precise Clock*, the work by Salazar Mendoza that popularized the mechanical clock with spiral balance wheel in New Spain. Since De Salazar had declined the invitation to be seated, the men remained standing, full of discomfort. The atmosphere was dense and their tension was tangible in every particle. The very flame of the lamp retracted into the silence that fell from time to time. All of Policarpo de Salazar's reasoning gave evidence of the Jesuit education he had received from his tutor, to which he had added his own judgements, developed on his travels and those lonely nights when he argued with himself in pressing, perhaps torturous thoughts. Don Antonio, on the other hand, spoke with the mentality of a man of the Enlightenment, influenced nonetheless by the ideas of Athanasius Kircher.

After a lapse into silence, Hernán cleared his throat and De León y Gama spoke again: Such is the precise nature of numbers, we think above all that they walk hand in hand with the order of life, although we are the ones who govern them and reign over their abstract manifestation in our minds, even if they should escape our dominion from time to time...

Silence fell again, a dense silence. De Salazar moved from his place and took up an inkwell. He wrote a list of numerals on the paper:

111 111	33 (3 367) = 111 111
222 222	66 (3 367) = 222 222
333 333	99 (3 367) = 333 333
444 444	132 (3 367) = 444 444
555 555	165 (3 367) = 555 555
666 666	198 (3 367) = 666 666
777 777	231 (3 367) = 777 777
888 888	264 (3 367) = 888 888
999 999	297 (3 367) = 999 999

The mathematician looked at the numbers, intrigued. While you were speaking, the other said with his eyes resting nowhere, I have found the mechanism that conceives them: one must simply manipulate the first numbers of the count... How can that be?, show me, requested the scientist. And then the watchmaker pointed: 367, the multiples of 33 are 33, 66, 99, 132,... Then he vomited out a series of numbers and arithmetic operations that De León y Gama swiftly noted so as not to lose track of them.

My God!, the learned man exclaimed as he looked at the table, what a strange association.

Policarpo's eyes shone with the satisfaction of a tyrant's as he contemplated the extension of his dominions, his unsuspected power to subjugate multitudes. Hernán held back an Ave Maria and crossed himself halfheartedly with his sweaty hand. To make such calculations with the mind alone was, with all certainty, the work of Satan. It was a gift that the Evil One bestowed upon his servants in order to conquer the souls of more followers for the darkness. In the academy of San Carlos, the mathematician had heard of people capable of similar feats, but none came close to his in complexity: he was hypnotized before the parade of numbers produced by this visitor. He was frightened to see that chaos maintained such order.

Policarpo de Salazar, master of the situation, spoke up and pronounced, in his muffled voice: The descent from pure ideas to the torturous paths of man becomes the driving force of great abominations. He was a prophet of the ominous, elaborating enigmas for the tormented species that races down an uncertain path toward the light, desperate to sate its thirst. When a handful of sand, continued the calculist, slips between the fingers, in the tumbling of each grain begins and ends the agitation of great numbers.

Silence fell again. As the clockmaker had mentioned sand, De León y Gama opened the *Harenaria* that lay upon his table. The book proposed figures beyond the myriad and numbers of indescribable magnitudes, difficult to imagine. He showed it to the calculist. The *Harenaria* contained the notes of a bold mind that would engender outrageous ideas, like that of filling the whole universe with grains of sand so as to then calculate their number. Numbers that emanate from secret parts of the mind to plough through immensity. Yes, colossal numbers that evoke the weight of the eternal, a swoon before enormous shadows that the eyes cannot hope to take in. The calculist's gaze took on a disconcerting brilliance. There was no expression on his face. He was impressed by the idea, but he made it clear to the scholar that he was referring to something *else*. He clicked his tongue. His eyes turned the brilliance into depth: in it, the mist set a pattern, pointing to that place deep as silent caverns in which endless vertigos and strokes throb in the darkness: the abysmal dwelling of monstrosities whose blasphemies deafen mortal ears, even immortal ears, as the thunderings of wicked voices that pronounce figures greater than the infinite.

De León y Gama, mathematician by trade and Enlightened man par excellence, understood the message of this gaze. The numbers of the *Harenaria* were reduced to the size of ridiculous ants clumsily advancing over the land of mortals. He swallowed salty saliva, the saliva of vertigo. Everything spun in the periphery of his gaze as he foresaw the existence of things that the mind vomits up by instinct so as not to give in to madness.

Policarpo de Salazar broke the silence with gestures and words of departure. Before he left, he turned his eyes to the two men who stood there, disturbed. Standing on the threshold, after a long pause, he stated by way of goodbye: There are not so many stars.

THE INHABITANTS OF THE STREET OF GOOD DEATH WERE silent, sullen. It was the street of transformations down which the people hurried in search of the priests of the Plaza of San Pablo to request confession for their dying moments. The residents' eyes ignored the passer-by: lost in monotony, with no sign of life, they seemed to contemplate the insides of themselves, the part where there are no sleep-filled nights but only darkness, cavities in which they once stored the knowledge of pain, and now nothing. They were clouded windows reflecting faces without emotion. Faces of nobody.

At that time, the city of Mexico, capital of North America in New Spain, was a nest of thieves and serpents. The viceroyalty found itself on the edge of decadence. In the upper chambers, the nobility snatched at titles like birds of prey in a chorus of cawing. Governing was the viceroy Martín de Mayorga, knight of the Order of Alcántara, a man considered austere, a patron of the arts, and pious, but who ignored or seemed to ignore the ungodly administration of the jurisdiction that lay in the hands of his cohorts, or their robbery of the poor, who, as the most miserable, proceeded to rob each other. In the street, the people threw old, foul-smelling rags from the balconies of the high stories. From the low doors, they hurled broken pottery, dead dogs and cats. The plazas served as markets and butcheries: numerous dogs, many with mange, congregated there to clean up the scraps. In Plaza Mayor, slaves were bartered in despicable traffic. Among the puddles and mires flitted flies hoping to plant their larvae in fruits and fried foods that would later be sold. From the windows hung the clothes of the convalescents of contagious diseases. From the same windows fell bits of rotten wood over the heads of those who bought and sold below. Beggars, some blind and crippled, others dragging themselves along the ground, plead for charity in verse or displayed revolting ulcers or monstrous, swollen legs for all to see. The masses walked along almost nude, not only due to their meager wages, but also due to their vices and games of all natures, culminating in street brawls, which supplied prisoners for the jails and bodies for the cemeteries, or at least wounded men who would later become beggars.

Through the streets passed convicts destined for the noose, whipped on by the executioner of the Chamber of Crime or the Holy Inquisition. There passed criers of holy edicts, wandering circuses, and feasts for the functions of the Royal and Pontifical University. There passed severe clerics in dark cassocks, before whom the world knelt and bared its head. There passed carts and coachmen, Indians and mestizos, mulatos and people of other castes, calling out their wares to the four winds.

After the diurnal hubbub, darkness and silence reigned: the ghost of a spectral muteness drifted through the sleeping avenues, not yet lit, down which only madmen and drunkards dared to tread. Along the Street of Good Death, one could hear the nocturnal procession of the Rosary of Souls advancing to the peal of a dismal bell, begging pitiably that Paternosters and Ave Marias be prayed for the eternal rest of the dead.

On those very nights, inside his silent room, the clockmaker of Good Death (as those who knew him called him by that time) counted the seconds before sleep. One second. Two. Fifty. One thousand one hundred… From his bed he numbered the death rattles of time by the light of the candle that threatened to go out. The synchrony of the needle advanced in its angular motion, determined, toward death. But it did so in reverse, in the clock that

Policarpo himself had built and whose hands turned backwards as if attempting to recover lost time, a return to the youthful years when the state of nature smiles and caresses.

THE COUNTERCLOCKWISE PROGRESS OF THESE HANDS, this demented artefact that Hernán Cuevas had seen in De Salazar's workshop, was the reason rumors started to circulate in Plaza Mayor. Before the merchants, he claimed the clockmaker's gifts were owed to powers obtained with concoctions made by the idolatrous Indians in the vicinity of San Agustín de las Cuevas. He mentioned that in his workshop he had also laid eyes on malignant instruments, among them a pendulum that never stopped swinging: what better proof could exist of a pact with the Evil One? He claimed the clockmaker possessed a compass opened to just the right degree that, when he used it to trace a circumference, whoever looked upon it would die. According to the servant, within the clockmaker's power were rules of measurement and specially graduated cords to determine the closeness of the dead and the frightful Llorona. As if this were not enough, he attributed to him the possession of manuals in pagan languages containing numbers with which to invoke the demons of Legion. He knows of curses and infamies by which a man is condemned for all eternity, he said. His inventiveness went to root in the crude ears of the masses, humble people who listened to him and grew confused, since while some thought they saw in him the 'coming Antichrist,' others took him for a healer, a layer-on of hands. Some thought him a fallen angel, wrapped in a garb of flesh and bone. Others imagined he had returned from among the dead.

The scarce clockmakers of the day tried to draw from him his particular knowledge of time, and they bowed in respect when they succeeded in hearing him speak of the art of establishing periods, of the exact proportions between the parts of the *relox*, of the Analytics of measurement, including the instructions to create assemblages on a ruby carved at the axes, and to place the escape mechanism, whether as a wheel or a pendulum.

Cuevas was far from suspecting that his unmeasured words had a measure of reason: at the site of De Salazar y Hurtado's mental silence worked a secret clock whose hands approached the point of twelve midnight.

NOT IMAGINING WHAT HIS SERVANT WAS SPREADING FROM mouth to mouth through the plazas (he planned to take him as his secretary in short order), De León y Gama also thought of the clockmaker. He scrawled numbers at his table.

Mathematics and art are joined by intimate bonds, he told himself. Bonds knotted between themselves, palpable in the obscurity that shrouds men's sleep in darkness. De León y Gama perceived beau ty in the faint strokes of subterranean geome try, or in the abstract formulation of algebra. He drafted curves and worked away at the game of fluxions and the squar ing of curves evoked in New ton's *Tractatus*. He also set his attention upon astronomical events and the terrestrial atmo sphere, observing all things as if through a kaleidoscope: di versity in unity, unseen colors, excessive forms. He allowed himself to be drawn in from the start by the configurations that were gradually defined into the plans for the Palace of Mines, under Tolsá, a daring architect and sculptor who reincorporated into the ar-

chitectural tradition the basic elements of symmetry and proportion of the Greco-Roman past. Yes, señor, he upheld, Manuel
Tolsá is the artist capable of fusing mathematic coldness with
the subtle textures of art, thereby penetrating the walls laid for
humankind before the act of creation. Also belonging to the kaleidoscope were all things related to navigation and the defor-
mation of longitudes, a subject treated by José de Zaragoza and
by Diego de Guadalajara y Tello in his magazine *Various notifica-
tions and reflections conducive to the good use of clocks*, which appeared beginning in 1777. The clock and the science of navigation
formed an indestructible unit. De Guadalajara y Tello was a
master of Mathematics of the Royal Academy of San Carlos,
where the level of abstraction was elevated and the community
kept up to date with recent advances. The same could be said of
the Royal Seminary of Mining, a place of high mathematics, superior to those of the Pontifical University. The learned man saw
clockwork as a liberal art, and he concurred with De León's tastes
for proportion and symmetry. Both had their own opuscules and
investigations, and this was the extent of the relation between
them. De León y Gama had nursed the secret idea of meticulous-
ly classifying all the mathematical knowledge of the day, but he
would never do so: time is more prone to slip away than water or
sand.

Between his tireless coming and going to and from the Seminary of Mining, wrapped up in revisions and comments on scientific texts, books, and symbols, the mathematician took the time
to think on his two encounters with the calculist. The man's voice
was impossible to drag out of his memory. How had it become so
deep, so muffled? He meditated upon the monstrous entities that
the clockmaker had put forth, allowing for the risky notion that,
perhaps, they did not deserve the name of numbers. Although De
León y Gama could not compare to him in skill and speed, he was

an excellent manipulator of numbers on his own account. Applying the methods of Leibnitz, he was capable of reaching magnificent approximations of irrational numbers to several decimal places, among them, for example, the number π, which served him well for the analysis of the problem of the circle's circumference. In his second encounter with De Salazar, once their discussion had begun, the mathematician had recourse to draft a circumference, a perfect drawing he completed without the help of a compass.

The fascination of the circle lies not only in its shape, argued De León, but also in its center, the point from which all others that lie on its curve seem to flee, seeking to become equidistant from it and to attain the maximum symmetry known to man. The distance from each of them to that enigmatic center, he continued, possesses a relation that all the varied cultures glimpsed, since when the double of this distance divides the length of the closed curve, a marvellous number emerges, quintessentially hypnotic, the figure pursued with grueling effort by the ancients: from Athens to the pagan lands of Moors and Muslims it was longed for, just as in Florence and the highlands at the top of the world, do you know?, there where the terrible Chinese and Tartar dynasties took root, and we need not even imagine how it was pursued by the Egyptians, the Babylonians, the Chaldeans, all the same, passing down their dream to the Pythagoreans, the Gnostic Christians, even the mages, until it was finally proved that the Earth is round: the circle appeared again! Then it was demonstrated that the Earth rotates on an axis, the learned man explained, all that rotates drafts circumferences around the geometric center of the turning shape...

Ignorant of the mechanism by which to calculate such a relation, Policarpo requested of De León the numbers he must divide in order to attain the marvellous figure. The number of circles that can be drafted is infinite, the latter answered, to seek two quantities whose quotient generates our number would lead to a grave problem. He related that an approximation given by Archimedes was later improved by Tsu Chang of China four hundred years after the ascension of Christ. Chang reached a number that was only approximated, and imperfect (the learned man wrote on a sheet of paper): 3.1415929... which was not precisely the one he was looking for, as it was exact until the penultimate written figure. Besides, the number of existent decimals had to be infinite, and it was impossible to predict, in any way, the next one in the list. See here, Policarpo, if you are interested there is a useful mathematical technique to slowly calculate its decimals, invented not long ago by a German, although it is laborious and it demands calculations and more calculations to obtain each figure with precision, signalled the mathematician. Many calculations... That will pose no problem, the calculist thought with arrogance. An outline of the techniques of Leibnitz convinced Policarpo of the contrary. With the word 'calculation,' the mathematician referred to algebraic techniques and an equivalent of the fluxions of Newton. For the other, it was all numbers. After that surprise began his obstinacy to know these capricious numbers that, when divided, would give rise to the other, also unknown. He needed them before him, well defined, to them manipulate them in his way. De León y Gama issued his sentence: The impossible cannot be done. But the calculist was already thinking, not listening, not surrendering his ear to the world. He was beginning to sink into abstractions, into seas of savage numbers concealed inside him, searching for that which he was sure must exist. De León watched him walk away, his demeanor hard and full of caution: like an animal that has been mocked.

De León y Gama thought of what would have occurred if Archimedes has possessed that same ability to calculate in his mind.

Would his geometry and catoprics exist, his hydraulics? Would they have been lost in the ocean of figures, paying no heed to the menace of Marcellus, that Roman predator whom he valiantly combated with his science? The learned man speculated. He imagined a monstrous vision in which Galileo bellowed numbers of all proportions from the heights of a leaning tower, with the people of Pisa noting them down, driven mad. If he was sure of anything, it was that the relation of shapes with numbers is not gratuitous: it is impossible to find it out with only the shape or with only the number. Was he really sure? He shared in Policarpo's initial perplexity, so much so that on the cusp of night, after a dinner he barely touched, he felt the company of fine particles floating in the air: they entered his head through his eyes, through his ears, through anywhere they could.

BACK IN HIS LODGINGS ON THE STREET OF GOOD DEATH, THE calculist took up cords of varying lengths to wrap the edges of circles cut from wood. He knew the torture of uncertainty, and it was that torture that hid things within their true form, in pursuit of numbers inaccessible to the clumsy action of measuring: because to measure is merely to guess.

He wondered about algebra just as he sank into confusion over the geometry of the infinitesimal. This Leibnitz... But numbers were his life and he *would reach*, through numbers alone, with no sort of artifice, the enigmatic figure. The values that resulted from his mental calculations, the products of imperfect measurements, drew him toward a figure hardly greater than three, with diffuse decimals that varied just like his uncertainties. The scale of measurement was never quite adequate, he needed the cords not to catch along imprecise points of the gradation, but they insisted upon slipping or stretching. A cord, a trap. He sought to trap a number whose decimals danced macabre before fading into the harshness of reality. It was true that circumference governed time, just as it is a fact that the grains of sand in the hourglass are themselves toothed circumferences. The clockmaker longed for knowable and existent numbers like those of the restless sea within him, always within and never without, fleeing from the mind that tried to hold them captive. Geometry must be a lie. From that moment on, the act of calculating took on the dimension of a feverish desire, emerging from nothingness for the seeker of numbers, as he watched hidden tenacities in the twinkling flame whose light is so bright as to be blinding. He sensed the coming of figures manipulable by nature that would give way to ecstasy. Surely the mathematician knew many of them and wished not to reveal them. Soon he would draw them out, by force if necessary.

Circumference was a ruse of movement, illusion, or perhaps creation, perhaps so was time, concocted by a mind determined to distort reality. Yes: they were creations of deceit.

NEITHER POLICARPO DE SALAZAR NOR DE LEÓN Y GAMA suspected that, near the location of their brief encounters, just nine years before, a puzzling device had been assembled in secret. New Spain was a center for the creation of mechanical entities governed by cogs. Machines built for any purpose, as if vomited out of Leonardo's sketches. Artefacts for the manufacture of leather objects or for grinding grain. Or for the spinning required in the little factories and looms that competed with the hands of artisans, whose cogs worked together in swift movement. (Others ended their lives as mechanical abortions abandoned under lean-tos or melted, their metal reshaped into horseshoes.) This device, though, had already taken its form. It had been freed from its creator's mind and gained access to the material realm. The machine was born from a hive of madness, inner longing and torment. A mechanism capable of something that, perhaps, no one in North America could have imagined. Mere months were required for its maker to unravel in the universal laws the measurements of its toothed wheels and pins, cranks and other barely conceivable ingenuities that circled, rightly placed, around each assemblage. It looked like nothing seen before. A machine-monster configured, firstly, in the tide of a brain relegated to the regions of discovery between shadow and light. A mental construction of innovative structure and dimensions. An offspring formed alone. Its design began in silence and in silence it ended, sharing nothing with the crass hubbub of the place where it was built, near the nascent construction that would soon become the Palace of Mines.

OF ALL THE CRIMES THAT POLICARPO DE SALAZAR Y HURTADO committed in his life, only once did he spill blood.

In 1781, another year of the Lord for the prelates, the murderer began making incursions into the house of De León with the exclusive purpose, he assured him, of seeking instruction in fundamental questions of mathematics. The mathematician received him with enthusiasm, even as the clockmaker's character continued to provoke mistrust and perplexity within him. The only one who never acquiesced to the arrangement was his servant. Whenever he could, with a wide range of pretexts, he impeded access to De León y Gama and thereby to his figures, and thus he created around himself an aureole of pale yellow light that marked him as a prospect before the doors of Hades.

Aware that the rumors he spread on the streets neighboring that of Good Death had not achieved their desired effect, Hernán conceived of new tricks to fight against his enemy. His fear of the man's ways had transformed into venom (how he hated him!): he ended up carrying himself with the haughtiness proper to viceroys before the masses.

A certain morning, the mathematician searched among his papers for a few documents and notes written in his own hand. They did not appear. Without success, he ransacked his study from top to bottom, his house, even the corners of the patio. He snapped at Hernán that he too should search. They found nothing. Giving up the objects for lost, he sank into dejection. Not finding his notes, among which were his observations on the texts of Galileo, and those referring to the matter of the measurement of time, as well as his investigations into algebra in response to the problem of the roots of polynomials of any degree, he sank into a depressed lethargy that gradually consumed his body and spirit. The soul darkens even upon contemplating the foam of the sea: that of the learned man was saddened to see the jagged reefs upon which broke the waters of uncertainty. Hernán was aware of the sorry state of De León y Gama, and he thought it best for the fulfilment of his purposes. Yes, he himself had hidden the documents away from that place. He prepared a plan of blackmail that would destroy the clockmaker, exposing him as a common thief. He held tight to the hope that this would be the ideal pretext for the Chamber of Crimes to take note of his diabolical objects and send him to the gallows. He needed only hide the pages in a new place: the workshop of the calculist. Thus, he would rid himself forever of his learned master's unexpected student. He would act after the sun set.

On the night he had selected to put his strategy in motion, he impatiently awaited the wee hours of the morning. He departed and made his way toward a certain dirty, forgotten chapel, a refuge for sleepless beggars. There, under a plank of the worn-out wooden floor, lay the stolen pages. Not long later, he walked toward the Street of Good Death through the hanging darkness that veiled the street's cobblestones. His silhouette advanced like a sad soul, a ghost returning to its damp place in the niche of the forgotten. He chose the back part of the workshop, taking care not to make any noise that might give him away. He succeeded in sneaking in through a window, beside a table on which half-built clocks were strewn. He knew De Salazar spent his nights there, so he groped his way forward, running his hands over objects in the dark. He could hear the violent pulses of his heart. His hands shook. One false move and all would be lost, the clockmaker would open his eyes and then nothing would make sense: the defendant at trial might be himself. Hernán Cuevas remained there, immobilized, for several long, anxious minutes. Should he truly be there? He did not know for sure, but he was just one step away from his goal: all he had to do was hide the papers in the workshop and leave as quickly as he could. He breathed in and kept moving. An unseen object appeared out of nowhere in front of his feet, making him trip and then fall with all his weight as the papers flew from his hands. It was the container of leeches that had repulsed him before. The vessel shattered and the old man's extremities fell at the mercy of the vile creatures. His body, stunned and knocked down to the floor (he did not know for how long), only reacted upon feeling the bloodsuckers' mouthparts attaching themselves to his body through the gaps in his clothes. They were sucking out the liquid that gave him life! He twisted in pain and whimpered, horrified. His left leg was broken, as were the fingers of one hand. He soon heard footsteps. The light of a candle grew clearer and illuminated the nooks and crannies of the room, and then those of a cadaverous face. Policarpo drew near, the defeated members and muscles of the old man were unable to respond. A few unlucky leeches twisted on the floor in irreversible agony. The murderer glanced at them before casting his eyes over the scattered papers; finally, he concentrated on him. At that instant, the old man knew that his antipathy, his hatred for the calculist had been requited for some time. He was lifted up by the clockmaker's strong hands, which carried him to a corner beside the candle. De Salazar looked at the ceiling as if giving thanks, just as a pent-up fury played over his features. Then he laid his eyes upon the desperate man and, in his cavernous voice, pronounced: Tonight I will teach you to count.

He calmly prepared the objects necessary to deliver death.

He grabbed the old man and tightly tied his feet, he tossed the end of the rope over a wooden beam in the ceiling, and then Hernán Cuevas was trapped, hanging with his head pointing down. His enemy picked up the living leeches, placed them in their pail, and pushed the container just under the hanging man. With a kitchen knife, he made an incision on the old man's temple. He had chosen a vein from which to begin an unhurried process of bloodletting: one by one, thick drops of life fell into the bucket. They were easily distinguished, easily counted. The servant looked upon the blurred, inverted face of the man who greedily pronounced numbers while his consciousness gradually fused with a circle drafted behind the murderer's back. He died slowly as he listened to the figures progress toward his own death.

The parasites in the bucket writhed gluttonously in the fresh blood. De Salazar y Hurtado was exhausted by the excitement. He looked over the content of the papers littered on the floor: among them were algebraic equations. He looked at the rigid corpse. He spent the rest of the night in the task of dividing up the useless body such that a numeric relation should be found between the number of pieces and the drops of life he had counted. With great care, he placed the parts in an ixtle sack. Still before dawn, he set out for Plaza Mayor and, among the rotting guts of pigs and cattle, he tossed the fragments of his victim. The bravest dogs, or the hungriest, nibbled on the sack with their desperate jaws. As dawn broke, they devoured the old man's mangled remains, below a sun that emerged red over the horizon: like blood.

POLICARPO LEAFED THROUGH THE MATHEMATICIAN'S PAPERS at night.

He held in his hands an indecipherable and hypnotizing mystery. The manuscripts marked the entrance to his warped learning, shaping his ingress to new nightmares. He learned the rudiments of algebra, which he considered vile just as he took them up with fascination. The dreams of reason began to produce monsters, dislocated visions before the candle that illuminated the yellowing pages. Alone, the murderer seemed full of life, his features lit up as he let out intermittent whistles of pleasure and also of pain. Each of the manuscript's claims made the calculist blink, uniting, as if carelessly, the iniquitous world of ideas with that of matter. Much of what happened after was owed to the incorrect conception that, from the abstract, this somber man developed. In his reading of De León's papers he found an annotation that read: *In algebra, a number is a common thing: algebra generalizes the number.* Then came an outline, in De León y Gama's style, of the theory of equations and generalized properties of numbers, now substituted by letters. Later he explained quadratic equations before delving into the techniques of Tartaglia and Cardano for those of the third order. The text was rich in details: it seemed that the pages were ordered systematically to make up a book. De León y Gama analyzed the solution of second order equations by square roots and an Arabic trick through which he reached, again, the same response. *Algebra, in its sovereignty, simplifies the things of life, it is not concerned with the necessities that rob it of cheer*, the text claimed. De Salazar shut his eyes with a combination of repulsion and devotion. The conglomeration of equations brought on opposite and contradictory sensations in him, jolts of nonsense that opened cracks and doors in his mind and then bashed against them with violence. One of these doors remained open: can an equation be solved using not algebra, but some kind of numerical intuition, an *algebra of the mind* with no need for paper nor *letters*? Worn down by the fatigue of his vain attempts, he remained sitting for many nights before the papers. Soon his head fell victim to violent pulsations on whose limits his mind wandered, thinking and then dreaming. On a wall, beside the skeleton of the *Polyptych of Death*, he painted symbols after choosing at random a striking equation from the notes of Antonio de León: $x^2 - 3^3x + 3^3 = 0$.

And so, time plunged him into misfortune. Little by little, the form that his gradual drowning would take became clear. As time passed by, he calculated furiously in his mind, sometimes for days at a time, desperate to discover the solution to that strange equation without the loathsome use of algebra. He found nothing. He was growing sick and pale. In his frustration he dredged up spiritual miseries, malevolent and sorry thoughts, every source of his shame. He stayed by the lit candle and stared at the *equation*, as the leaves of the calendar drifted past and fell cyclically from the tree of time. He thought beside the Cathedral, in the plazas, and outside the leprosariums. The troubling and dry form of the *equation*, the time he passed impassibly, and those tormentous and invisible numbers, day by day and night by night, marked his face. The people of the city bumped into him, the clockmakers, the colliers, women who sharpened knives and scissors, cartwrights and children: he was a shadow without a body to cast it. All avoided him and continued on their paths.

De Salazar y Hurtado abandoned clocks forever. In his room, he concentrated his mind again and again beside the candle. Time was gradually consumed in that flame that shone and, pallid, burned. The mathematician asked after him with no success.

Although the mathematician's notes pointed out the infinity of similar equations, he continued to concentrate on that equation alone. He dared to cross seas of numbers, waterfalls of figures upon figures in the daily labor to which he submitted his head until it almost burst. That was when he felt countless waves of vertigo pressing him toward formless precipices, into which heads no longer capable of producing ideas are tossed like hollow nuts that, upon crashing against the ground, reveal their emptiness and roll downhill until they are crushed. In vain, he tried to feel his way through the void with his blind survey, a sticky void, his *algebra of the mind*. He recognized the face in the mist before he even looked upon it: first before the circle, now faced with solving the equation. His pursuit of baseless illusions, without reflection, had left him disappointed. He told himself: The world is a vile mirage (in his devastation he pronounced the word *vile* for the first time). He was seen alone on the bridges, especially at night. *He was counting things*, said his neighbors on the Street of Good Death. He faced the terror of nothingness! Policarpo's face had changed, his skin looked like wood dried out and ground down by time. Old Hernán had died years ago, and the dogs had surely swallowed his remains, but the servant's vengeance had been consummated from the depths of Hades. This destruction was worse than the one he had planned, and it had already taken its seat on the throne of doom. At the end of his fascination, having made the efforts of a titan of the mind, the years escaped him and all he discovered were sad, diffuse, incomplete numbers.

He had no choice but to fill this emptiness with the presence of himself and return, a prodigal son, to his elemental numbers. The number is taken from reality, he thought in his room, and not from spectres. I must go out onto the streets to find them, he finally declared aloud. At that moment, he felt like himself again and he began again his life's work. There exists an incommunicable joy in enumerating the signs of a life that flickers between the fingers as it disappears.

PEOPLE FEAR DARKNESS, AND ALSO LIGHT. AT THE END OF 1789, a troubling light appeared at night in the heavens. Its phosphorescence arched across the whole of the celestial vault, terrifying the inhabitants of the city of Mexico. No one could explain the source of the glow, which evoked that of a ghost. It robbed the stars of their shine. It defied the moon. The phantasmagoric light hung from the heights, like luminous liquid spilled across the sky, washing away the breath of souls. On those nights of terror, the glow froze the bones, it gave pause to many hearts like a gust from the sidereal distance, an omen of the end, the gaze of God awakening from a deep sleep, about to witness the sin of souls: eyes that contemplate all, down to the deepest depth, to then pass judgment with the wrath of ages.

Few left their homes. The old women whimpered after forgetting the words of their prayers. The children were wrapped up completely in blankets and garments of wool, while their parents begged the heavens for the return of shadow. Sobbing with remorse, men relinquished their vices like dirty rags of clothing, left lying on the ground. Women abandoned their gossip and minded their tongues as they anxiously clutched their scapulars. They ceased copulating with their husbands and placing their hands between their thighs when they were alone. The noble ladies, wives of miserly creoles, lost their fat as they forgot their gluttony, fearfully abandoning their sweets and their prized *chocolatl*. More than a few scattered ashes on their beds and knelt on grains of rice that cut into their knees in their vehement prayers. Others gave to charity and dressed in the garb of the poor, punishing their bodies. All began to clothe themselves in an aura of sanctity: their beatitude stank, an uncunning sign of hypocrisy, emerging from the anxious desire for a redemption that was distant and longed-for nonetheless, like the urge of the sufferer of thirst to drink sour wine or seawater, or blood, whatever it might be to survive. And so, the souls flapped their arms in an effort not to sink like castaways into their misery. In some places, *prophets* emerged. The helpless hurried down the path to the Sanctuary of Guadalupe, the other temples and chapels filled as well, and within them hymns were heard, intoned with fervor. Every priest was an incarnation of hope: the clergymen were embraced with despair among seas of candle bearers whose flames flickered in a sad, icy draft of wind, slipping through the cracks in the church roofs. On those luminescent nights, the temples' doves nested close and cooed softly, they flew over the nearby rooftops offering a sinister spectacle: not a sign of peace but a warning that they would devour the bodies of those fallen in judgment, like the carrion birds they really are. The beggars pointed to the sky with their monstrous and deformed extremities as they cursed and cast scornful gazes at the world. Arachnids and vermin scuttled uneasily from the cracks and splits in the walls. Scorpions were seen linking their pincers in pairs: they performed a danse macabre under that stream of light, overflowing from the Milky Way and from the stars.

This unpredictable happening in the heavens affected the minds of the learned just as it did the superstitious. Few were the individuals who stayed standing and searched through the scientific method for the causes of the incident without placing their own fears in between. One such individual was De León y Gama, who elaborated his own theory regarding the phenomenon, a dissertation based on the theory of the ether, which was, in his judgment, influenced by the moon: *The moon is the agent that places in motion and agitates the ether*. It was unknown whether the phenomena of the aurora borealis took place within the atmosphere or above it. De León y Gama argued that the aurora occurred on top of the atmospheric layers. Then another theory emerged, proposed by the physicist and meteorologist J. Francisco Dimas Rangel: he claimed that a certain electrical agent was inflaming the atmospheric matter. In time, it would be revealed that Dimas Rangel was closer to the truth. In the meantime, the unlearned people clamored, trembling and fearful, under that "fire on the horizon."

In those very days, in the streets, in the little plazas, and under the bridges, they began to find cadavers with ashen faces. On the petrified features of the corpses was a look of terror, but they had not died of fear: they had been strangled. The evidence of their suffering persisted in their contracted, twisted tongues, and in the eyes, standing out of their sockets, of those victims snatched abruptly from life. The fear they inspired was owing, in part, to one fact: they seemed to continue staring into the cause of their death.

DON FERNANDO MANGINO WAS INFORMED OF THE EVENTS by the viceregal police. Until then, the administration at his command (by order of De Angulo y Bodoquín himself, knight of the Order of Calatrava) had made manifest that he could continue to serve at the viceroy's right hand for a long time, thereby legitimizing his popularity as a leader. Now, something frightful was happening in the streets.

On the Street of Firewood, a man was found with an atrophied throat and a sunken Adam's apple. The people had cried out in terror: the dead man, his mouth open, gave the impression of begging with a grimace of anguish for the air that he would never breathe again. His vision was frozen in the act of watching death, and on his lips was the intense violet paint of swelling blood. The cadaver's fingers were terribly twisted, all of him was. After two days, on the Street of the Basque Women, an old woman was found. Just the same, the mark of asphyxiation levitated over her face. Her bloodshot eyes seemed to bulge out of their sockets. The woman had been strangled several hours before, and her little body, shrunken, displayed the rigidity of those who will not rest even in death. The police noted in their report to Don Fernando Mangino that the old woman had foam around her mouth, emphasizing the fact that around her flimsy neck, bruised and uncovered, hung a little image of the Virgin of Guadalupe with her palms together and her face of peace, of warmth, so different from the disfigured visage of the poor victim.

Thick mist blew past under the light of the sky that had caused so much clamor in past days. Fear remained in the city with another face. A skeleton intoned funeral songs on the alleyways and bridges, it was time to pray not to become one of those breathless bodies that appeared on the streets. The shadows, the lights, the murmurs of the city, the hustle and bustle: all the sounds had become phrases of the melody that death sings to men as she works, with her cold and bony hands, the spinning wheel of what is to come.

It did not take long for more bodies to appear. A young woman. Then two men. Whoever killed them did so with a surprisingly measured violence, blending cold blood with the fortitude of a murderer breathing in the darkness. Soon there was no shortage of deaths in the vicinity. The suspense of the people. The bodies were discovered in chapels, nibbled by the dogs on rubbish heaps, sometimes in the fountains.

Once they are submerged in the mist, the look of absence on the dead is accentuated. But the rigid cadavers that were dragged off the pavement resembled living, tortured statues, which might at any moment let loose the scream trapped in their throats. Fernando Mangino crossed himself in secret when he thought of those contained screams, whose echo had flooded the city. For the first time, the people heard the canticle of the defleshed beings whose eyes remain all too open, never to close. De Angulo y Bodequín, the gentleman viceroy, ordered inquiries and searches with no result as the rage against his men increased. He was a pitiless man, an expert in contempt, especially toward the Indians. With the arrogance of a man with military matters firmly in his grasp, he publicly vociferated and described cruel punishments, with the hope of causing fear in the criminal. The Court of the Holy Office, for its part, pronounced a sentence: in their dictates they mentioned the rack and other instruments of torture that awaited silently in damp cellars and dungeons.

The waves of homicide continued. Sometimes they ceased for a month or more. Then they returned like inevitable tides. The victims appeared at dawn under the Bridge of Jesus, the Bridge of Mercy, that of Juan the Collier, that of the Bishop, and others with no name. Sometimes they were dredged out of the canals those bridges crossed. From under the Bridge of Jesus they pulled a fragile little boy, who in his misfortune had met the same sort of death. Infuriated, Don Fernando Mangino read the report. The child had a rope knotted with such force around his neck that the doctor assigned to cut it, even with all his skill, could not help but slice into the tender throat, from which dark blood slowly trickled.

A prisoner of his impotence, Mangino persistently offered rewards of jewels to whomever might provide useful clues to catch the murderer. Just the same, noble titles were promised to the dirty, ignorant people to make them participants in the pursuit. Spreading news of the impious crimes through printed media was prohibited on pain of death: not only did they expose the administration of the viceroy to critique and scepticism, they jeopardized his authority throughout New Spain. It was the last thing the maximum hierarch needed: that the fingers of a vulgar killer, in the words of De Angulo y Bodoquín, should put at risk his continuity in power. The panic of the nobility grew when, near the property of the viceroy, the body of a certain nobleman was found, the Baron De Santillana y Cosme, who had been gagged with great thoroughness: his mouth was full of rags and paper: on this occasion the murderer decided not to wring the throat: with only two fingers, he squeezed the nostrils and asphyxiated the unfortunate Baron De Santillana. To the viceroy's good fortune, the scandal that such a death should have caused was stifled by the notice of the sudden death of Carlos III, the king of Spain. The knight of the Order of Calatrava demanded of the people that they mourn his death and threatened any who disobeyed with severe fines. The people did not forget their concern over future crimes.

On days like these, the Inquisition's noose, that rope dangling from the gallows on its wooden post, was no more than a risible and absurd symbol.

DOGS HOWLED IN THE STREETS AND FAR AWAY THE CLOCK of the cathedral could be heard to strike eleven at night.

The storehouse was sunken in a peaceful silence, softly interrupted by the clinking of the golden coins that Doña Gertrudis counted intently. Thanks be to God, her earnings of the day exceeded those of the day before. The idea of dedicating herself to the grain trade had borne fine fruits, all the more because she was able to conduct the matters of her business by intuition until becoming wealthy. The grains were bought for laughable prices and were sold at a profit margin of triple their cost. Once the business was operating successfully, Doña Gertrudis threw out her anodyne husband, who lacked ambition, to administer the trade alone. Every grain was weighed and reweighed, never a coin more than needed was let slip. Corn, beans, barley, peanuts, and amaranth arrived, but she also received condiments like sesame, oregano, and cloves that were carried on the backs of mules or on the sweating shoulders of Indians. The people of the lowest classes were the first to receive the harshest deals from the witch, who compensated them for their grains at her pleasure (if at all), as she had the habit of paying only on rare occasions: she did so by extorting the unfortunates, assuring others, always in public, that they were delinquents who had robbed her. She typically brought along a *witness* such that the people, in their humble and fearful condition, ran off empty handed, hearing the thick woman's roars of laughter behind their backs. And so, the chests of grain overflowed like the sea to provide the city's outskirts. The rest stayed where it was to supply the nobles and the well-to-do.

Coated in sweat, the coins passed through untrustworthy hands time and time again. Doña Gertrudis noted down figures on lined paper. The echo of gold on a night spent alone is the most beautiful music to the miserly ear. The woman yawned, satisfied. She counted grains and money. With this fortune, she would be well able to procure the company of a man to revive her passions. She liked them young and robust. And besides, if the world was to end soon, she was happy to let others worry about it: people of little will and imagination, worth nothing. With warmth in her eyes, she cast a final glance over her precious crowns. She yawned again. She sat surrounded by a sweet, enveloping lethargy, in which it would be easy not to notice that from the shadow a human figure emerged, its face covered. There was no time to react. A knife slit her throat and from it burst abundant streams of liquid that would never return. The woman shook her wide arms, she tried to scream but she could only let out vague, muffled whimpers. She still had time to doubt the reality of what was happening: she remembered the being that was so feared on the streets, but he strangled and this one had cut her throat. Her effort to see the silhouette's face was entirely useless. Everything else began to lose its shape, life slipped away from her too fast. She succumbed under her own weight. The oil lamp fell at her side and shattered as she babbled and drowned in her own blood. Then the rest of the world transformed into darkness and went blank. In total silence, when the act was consummated, the faceless man departed into another darkness: that of a night without stars.

IT IS NOT UNCOMMON FOR EVIL TO BE NOURISHED BY THE fog of legends.

A century and a half before these crimes, midway through 1612, a Spanish knight trod the lands of New Spain, a man of Burgos, known as Don Juan Manuel de Solórzano. He arrived with the party of Diego Fernández de Córdoba, the Marquis of Guadalcázar. Besides possessing much wealth, the gentleman knew how to make friends in the high circles of the nobility, he dominated many subjects and had a gift for words like few others. From his arrival, he was afforded respect thanks to the composure with which he conducted business and, years later, when Lope Díaz de Armendáriz found himself in the seat of power, the latter showered him with homages and favors, a fact envied by enemies and kin alike. Some time later, the man met Doña Mariana de Laguna, a fine and virtuous woman. Flattered by her promising looks, he decided to propose marriage, to secure his ideal of joy and happiness. He established their residence near that of Lope Díaz. The friendship became a brotherhood and the viceroy offered Don Juan the administration of the branches of the Royal Estate, an important post administered by the Audience, whose members were displeased by the hierarch's decision. Conspiracies spread and the Audience threatened popular uprisings, just as humiliating rumors circled around the figure of Lope Díaz.

In 1640, the revolt in Catalonia distracted the attention of Felipe IV from his viceroy's administration of Mexican territory. The authorities of the city of Mexico, who had taken offense at the viceroy's actions, saw the opportunity to take revenge on Lope Díaz de Armendáriz and, at the same time, on the hated knight. The latter disappeared from sight. Here, history begins to blend with myth. Legend ever conforms and integrates words with rumors. Among those offended by the knight's success was one who now served as Minister of Crime: Francisco Vélez de Pereira. Taking advantage of the distracting Catalan uprising, Vélez de Pereira immediately called for Don Juan to be taken captive and led to a dark, foul smelling cell. There hell began. From there, the monotony was accompanied for days by the sounds of the rats sniffing around the corners of the cell in search of the bread that was tossed to the prisoner. The knight tried to take in the facts and understand his circumstances, as he was kept up to date with what was taking place beyond his heavy bars. One night, his most trusted informant brought him news that closed in around him and lashed him viciously: Doña Mariana de Laguna, his wife, was having relations with the Minister, the same who had locked him away, confined in darkness. Blinded by jealousy, the wounded man lost his reason, overcome by frustration and a terrible rage. It is said that he bellowed in pain and writhed on the hard surface of his cot. He swore vengeance. In his desperation, he turned to a wealthy and influential friend, Don Prudencio Armendia, who succeeded in freeing him from prison. Don Juan Manuel de Solórzano immediately made his way to the home of the unfaithful woman. Chance set the scene for him to find her in the arms of his enemy. Consumed by rage, he charged at the Minister and killed him with great violence before his terrified wife, whose screams could be heard throughout the street.

When the truth of a fact is entirely unknown, new words emerge, governed by laws that attempt to reconstruct it, to delve into the unseen and penetrate into the very base of the events. This is why another version of what occurred exists. It is said that the knight, in spite of his wealth and his social position, held a deep pain in his innards, as his beautiful wife had not given him heirs. How disgraced he thought himself! He sought solace in religious practices, he spent days at the churches trying to see the golden light of God under their domes. He felt the call of the habit to such an extent that he sought separation from his wife and considered devoting himself to the order of Saint Francis. This was the reason he disappeared from sight. In this presentation of the fact, Francisco Vélez, the Minister of Crime, goes unmentioned, although it does make reference to a lover kept by the wife. De Solórzano found out about his existence. Neither the love of God nor his Franciscan precepts could keep the serpent of jealousy from nesting in the man's heart. In the end, he cast his habit to the floor, shut himself away from his social sphere and, alone in his room, he began to rot with hate. He knew not the lover's identity, but he aimed to kill him. A prisoner of his delirium, he directed his supplications to the demons of hell. A certain night, he heard a voice that spoke to him, he knew not whence it came. The speaker said he would accept his soul in exchange for the information he requested. He gave him his first order: that very night, he must go out when the clock struck eleven and kill, in the darkness, the first individual who crossed his path. The knight obeyed. He smiled, satisfied, until he heard the cavernous voice again. The dead man is not guilty, he heard, you must go out on other nights to kill and continue until I show myself again beside the body of the true culprit. From then on, wrapped up in a dark cape after pronouncing blasphemies, the knight awaited his victims. When a passer-by approached, he walked up to the person, asking: Forgive me, my lord, what is the time? They gave him the time. From between his garments he drew a keen dagger, whose glitter made the unhappy target throw up their hands, and after pronouncing, *be happy, my lord, to know the hour at which you die!*, he leapt like a gust of wind upon his victim and drove the knife home.

The dawn surprised the petrified city. From the street, the morning rounds picked up corpses, with no one able to explain these frightful crimes. The knight's thirsty soul was not sated until fate took a turn against him and one morning, devastated, he learned that among the victims lay a nephew of his whom he had loved dearly. He sobbed with remorse. Again, he heard voices calling him. Soon he began to see horrible visions. One night he could bear them no more, and he let them lead him toward the plaza, to his fatal destiny (surely planned by the Devil). The next day he was found hanging from a rope, his face distorted.

HIDDEN, INSPIRED BY THE WAVE OF CRIMES THAT HAD LONG suffocated the city of Mexico (more strangled corpses would appear), a jackal, a lean, dirty wolf began his own chain of murders that carried on shockingly from the first: not satisfied to see death caused by *another*, he felt the selfish urge to act himself and to be feared. He killed in the style of the gentleman from a century before, Don Juan Manuel de Solórzano. In the complicity of shadow, the individual huddled in unsuspected corners and waited. Those who were led by accident toward him met the knife. Like the subject of legend, before he surprised them with the steel, he asked them for the time. Then he sank the blade deep, many times, or he slit their throats. This murderer enjoyed spilling blood, aware of how he troubled with viceroy's guards and the people. The streets bore witness as he fled the scenes of his crimes, but, mute, they kept the secrets of his nocturnal routes. Occasionally the man entered houses and killed inside. The city was dyed red. The blood began to clot. Horror mixed with confusion and the police scoured the streets searching for bodies. There were no clues, no signs of light to guide their pursuit: only corpses. The members of the court argued, they alleged that the murderer had changed his ways and now used not only the rope but also the knife. Or, perhaps, there was *another*. A priest observed at Sunday masses that the morality and cleanliness of the soul had disappeared.

Ungodliness showed forth like a clap of thunder. An emergency curfew was put in place. With great despair, mothers brought their children into their houses while the sun still shone. Blood called for blood, the people were stabbed, slit, if not strangled or terrorized (terror is a slow death). A spectre trod the avenues, flooding them with a warm and ample bath of blood. It was the month of October.

ALONE, IN HIS ROOM, HE IGNORED THE WORLD AND ALL THE spheres that hung about it. He merely drafted his numbers: De Salazar y Hurtado.

Months had passed, then years. Serene, Policarpo contemplated the numbers he had collected exception: the numbers. All were beautiful, without exception: the numbers of the final fuel of life. On the street, the people still groaned, the press still kept silent and, by high orders, the court feigned blindness. Individuals suspected of the crimes were locked up in dungeons, their hands were amputated by saw, but the strangling continued just as blood was still spilled by the feared knife. The work of the other criminal mattered little to Policarpo, each followed his own path and walked along the edge of his own abyss. At heart, though, he was bothered: the guards patrolled in greater numbers now, and he was forced to take greater precautions. On the plazas, the tradesmen were wrapped up in debates regarding the murderers, comparing them to each other, and even the youngest opined over which was more ungodly and pitiless. Two faceless darknesses filled the mouths of vulgar folk.

Policarpo had cut himself off from the world for another reason: three months before, as he rounded the lazar houses in search of potential victims, he had picked up the contagion so justly feared by the masses. When he went out, he had to cover his face and clothe himself in the loose garb of a woman. With bits of leather, he constructed a pair of crude gloves to cover the dirty white pustules on his hands. Neighbors and those who watched him walk by thought he was the *old lady* of the clockmaker. They paid him no mind: it had been so long, that shadow had blended into the silhouettes of forgetfulness. At his bench, he reviewed the deaths he had inflicted. His course of action was well defined. He went out in the wee hours of the morning when the guards' heads were nodding after their rounds. No one thought he would kill when the nascent sun was only just beginning to tinge the darkness with hints of light. When it was possible, he did it in the night, or in the day in some remote chapel where solitary penitents prayed. In his delirium, he once grasped the neck of a statue of Saint Teresa. He imagined the twisted, contorted face of the holy woman. The dirty prints of his hands remained, outlined on the martyr's frozen neck. The gasps were important, or the number of them and the pleasure, in and of itself, of listening to them in the silence. When it happened (and the pincers of his hands took action), he shook his head from side to side, his veil slid off and his victims stared into his hideous face. De Salazar knew not that the other criminal also hid his face, but while no one looked upon the other's face at the moment of death, they always looked into his. At times, the police came in time to see Policarpo as dawn broke: thanks to his feminine attire, his ample undergarments and his shawl, they took him for a kind old woman, and on more than one occasion they advised her to go with caution.

The authorities promised the criminals would soon be captured. Sooner or later all the wicked fall, they assured, like thieves caught red-handed in the night, and it was high time for this pair to do so. The storm was followed by moments of calm. A tranquility, just as ominous, in which he plotted and *experimented* with the deathly figures he had accumulated over the years on sheets of rag paper. If anyone had seen Policarpo, they would have thought him a messenger of the underworld manipulating the numbers of the judged on the Last Day. His figures let out their own pitiful racket as, under the deforming flickers of the candle's flame, they flooded and stifled the clockmaker's room. A sea of mud and confusion trembled in the room, the unwilled or perhaps willed insanity of the mind, perhaps that of an age that kept its tremendous frustration to itself. De Salazar y Hurtado was a sleeping being, letting out deep sighs from its shapeless dream, on the shore of the earthly chasm. He inhabited a space forgotten by men and the elements, unwhole before the night, condemned to misfortune and immobilized by great chains laid by other hands. In his mind was chaos, numbers without reasoning, the deceit of shapes and of a geometry in which his feet met no ground. On the other hand were clocks in their eternal pendular swing, the pendulum that makes equal the rocking of a baby and the rocking of a strangled man. In the whole, shaken by chance, he searched for the means to unify the parts. From the number, he sought its conjunction. The shapes with the number, the world with the number and time and life, but easier were death and the number only as an element of unification. The number was as cold as he, and yet it said so much every time. His preference for the disproportionate made him whole and was inextricably able to help him glimpse the beauty negated by reality. This was why the *Polyptych of Death* hung on his wall. Within him lodged a mutilated artist. Perhaps the shape could have been his supreme goal, or the symbolic and abstract world foreseen in the *equation*. And yet, the number still belonged to him. The figures before him were his own, as were the last breaths of suffocation that resonated in the cavities of his brain.

His skill as a calculist allowed him to establish complex and intricate relations between the figures of horror. He had filled books with these connections, many of them just as surprising as the one he had written years earlier before the eyes of De León y Gama, the mathematician. And so his dreams, now measured by the clock in reverse, now menaced by the interior movement of the gears of another mechanism (a mysterious machine manipulating figures), began their flight toward perdition.

ONCE FINISHED, THE MACHINE REMAINED FOR TWO MONTHS in the power of its maker, who marvelled himself at the fact that it worked. This had occurred in 1772, while Policarpo de Salazar wandered through the lost settlements of Puebla, among swindlers and beggars, not yet planning his return to the city of Mexico. The inventor, who would have never imagined that someone could calculate with the skill of Policarpo, felt the thirst to be immortal. To exit his anonymity, which only brings obscurity and silence, he revealed his work that same year before a group of ghosts with an aura of sapience. His machine manipulated numbers. Anguish and ecstasy, a fully argued case, the spasms of love for a certain science seemed to shine there in all their splendor, contouring the gears of the spinning wheels. Every roller turned with precision, communicating its momentum to every other in the form of numerals. The *Calculating Wheel* was presented by its creator in the following terms:

> Secure in the knowledge that Mathematics holds in all her treatises abundant and exquisite manual demonstrations, with which she certifies the truth of her rules, and observing arithmetics devoid of a manual instrument that serves as testament to its doctrine, as the mother gives milk to the first rudiments for the coming of that prodigious Science, I offer this *Calculating Wheel* in which not only is the demand for any account absolved with the greatest naturality, but the foundation and root of the number is made visible, which is the point.

The device added, subtracted, multiplied, and divided, as well as operating with fractions. It was designed to reach figures on the order of hundreds of millions. The chroniclers made note of the event, and their testimony lies in the National Library of Madrid at catalogue number 18744:

> Explanation of an arithmetic instrument invented in Mex-
> ico, year 1772, which can be given the name of...

The *Wheel* was questioned by members of the Holy Office. Theological writings were found containing arguments, behind closed doors, regarding the moving parts within the mechanism: tormented souls from Purgatory, mysteriously forced to work the figures by the artefact, by the Devil himself, or by some pagan spirit of the Hebrew Kabbalah. How could this machine put man to shame, take his place in the tasks of the mind, those gifts of Providence? The Jesuits, on the contrary, showed optimism, pointing out that Roger Bacon had dreamed of similar artefacts for the benefit of man: wondrous machines able to elevate the human to unsuspected realms, and it must be noted that Bacon was thoroughly devoted to the Lord...

Meanwhile, Pascal and his invention, a machine similar to the *Wheel* (although it could only add) but created decades prior, slept forgotten in old Europe. The *Wheel* was discreetly confiscated by the church. Those who knew of its existence, including its inventor, received threats. The artefact was locked away in a cellar of the Inquisition, alongside diverse instruments of torture. Among the faithful, there were some who stealthily peeked their heads into the cellar and gazed at the machine in terror as they thought of the torments the mechanism must inflict. The invention was later moved to other places, until its was decided to place it on a ship to Spain, where its fate would be decided. The ship charged with its transport had long sailed the seven seas, it was a vessel as old and rickety as the world to which it was sent. The crude sailors placed the *Wheel* in a corner of the ship's wooden belly, among barrels of oil, provisions of rope, and blankets. The craft reached the dock of Cádiz, where the crew drank wine and became drunk at the sight of their homeland. The men forgot to unload the *Wheel*. The ship was sent to the Canary Islands on another commercial expedition. It traveled to Africa, past Morocco and Tangiers. It skirted the coast of Asia. The ship's captain decided to venture to the Philippines and, at his own risk, to reach Japan, in an intrepid attempt to do business with the Japanese, who maintained their island in total isolation from the world: the *sakoku*, imposed from 1639 by the Tokugawa shogunate. The vessel was seen off and its crew deafened by thunderclaps of Japanese gunpowder. The captain embarked on the sorry return and the ship traipsed across the aquatic immensity until reaching the Antilles, it sailed the waters of the Caribbean on several commercial expeditions and then made way with its prow pointing north, where it finally ran aground on the coasts of the Yucatán, with its wood worn through, eaten away by sea salt and time. The captain, already bent with age, rediscovered the artefact in the ship's hold. He left it in the hands of the local Franciscans who, blind and ignorant to what lay before them, sent the device to the city of Mexico. The machine returned to its birthplace on the twenty-eighth day of September of 1794, after sleeping at sea for twenty-two years. Those who had condemned it, those old priests with the nose of a fox, were long dead. The old city was now another.

No one knew how the artefact worked, its presence there was a synonym of strangeness. From the Pontifical University it was carried to the halls of the new viceroy who had recently taken the throne: Miguel de la Grúa Talamanca y Branciforte. In the royal chamber, engineers, mathematicians, and other thinkers were brought together by the powerful man himself, who was anxious to hear the news of the machine. Yes, that he might at least reach an understanding of the purpose of the numbers on its toothed wheels: perhaps it was a *mechanical kalendar* that could be usefully installed in the audience chamber. No one could make it work.

One morning, a small and insignificant old man knocked on the viceroy's door. He claimed to be the inventor. The guards mocked the man who, nonetheless, requested to be led to the machine. Branciforte was surprised to see him manipulate the artefact with skill, after polishing it and repairing an assemblage that had been broken when the ship ran aground. All marvelled at his feat and applauded, as if before a circus spectacle. The old man asked for numbers at random and operated with them. Others carried out the calculations by hand and verified the results, some of which required hours of figuring. The machine did it in seconds! The viceregal hall lay open for a week to the curious, that they might admire the invention and appreciate the viceroy's generosity. Clothed in a garb that let him pass unnoticed among those who watched the *Wheel*, with his face hidden by a shawl like those of the housemaids, useful for hiding his grimace of anguish, was Policarpo de Salazar y Hurtado.

SOMETHING HAD TREMBLED WITHIN HIM. HE WAS DISTURBED and paralyzed before the vision of a decomposing face that the mirror returned to him, a horrid reflection that crossed space to come back to him, cast off by the polished glass and his constructive hand. Or, rather, returned by the *kosmos*. That immemorial anathema devoured his flesh: invasive leprosy. Something more purulent, nonetheless, corroded the interstices in his soul so gravely that neither the pustules on his face nor their infection could equal it.

That nameless thing was deeper than his sleepless nights. De Salazar y Hurtado contracted his features in a sign of terror before the emptiness placed by destiny a single meager step before him. *Horror vacui.* He was about to tumble from the heights. In brief, his whole self would be consumed like an altar candle set apart from time and from men. He would disappear! The news of the calculating device struck him dumb until, in the viceroy's chamber, he was convinced of what they said. Not only did he witness its magnificence, he corroborated its calculating capacity himself. The old inventor said before the spectators that the principle of its workings was *quite simple*, unlike its range, as the colossal numbers it computed escaped the skill of any human mind. A machine that calculates, equipped for the art of numeric manipulation, and much swifter than man... that wicked being corrupted objects, changed the orders of existence, and, what was worse, dismembered perfection. Its gears were unlike those of the innards of the kindly clock: instead, they made up abominable, dangerous dentitions. The machine, that wicked *Wheel*, snatched something intimate within him forever. The darkness that hung over him encompassed the immense with its gigantic wings and descended upon him with the weight of infinity. His leper's breath misted over the mirror's glass while the second hand of the clock, monotonous, marked the coming of his sentence. And if the *Wheel* were capable of finding the number that he could not, the number that, without the artifice of algebra, was the definitive solution to the quadratic formula of his bewilderment, the *equation*? He felt panic. It was more than viable that he would be forever replaced. He had not slept for days. His life was disrupted and he stopped collecting numbers in the streets. No more lives cut short for the moment. He had to do something about the device, he thought to himself, a mechanism like that simply could not exist, not while he was alive. Besides, it was unthinkable to allow the existence of some *inhuman* thing that could surpass him and deprive him of his reason for being. He already knew hell by its flames, but there was another detail worthy of his misgivings: a few men of influence planned to have replicas built of the machine, they had the authorization of the nobility and it was only a question of awaiting the consent of His Lordship Don Miguel de la Grúa. That would be the end! His action was urgently needed, even if he had to murder the viceroy himself to reach the *Wheel*.

Before the mirror, he looked again at his face, and then at the *Polyptych of Death*. Then, with grief, he turned his eyes toward the equation that was the source of his anguish. Lastly, he saw his beloved numbers, copies of his own suffocation. He picked up a sheaf of papers and walked hurriedly out of his workshop. Above hung a clouded sky, black and damp, that weighed over the atmosphere of Mexico.

DE LEÓN Y GAMA HEARD SHARP RAPS ON HIS DOOR. WEIGHED down by the years, he lifted his body slowly to answer them. He was almost blind, and he held up the oil lamp in his right hand. It was raining buckets, and he doubted that anyone had really knocked, perhaps it was the sound of the storm. As he opened the door, he looked upon a body covered up in the clothes of a woman. His visitor's garments were wet, and he stood immobile. He laboriously raised the light toward the covered face: it was impossible to make out the features of the figure that stood before him. Under the folds of his garb, within its leather envelope, was a sheaf of yellowing, worn out pages, which he extracted from the protective covering and extended toward the man. They were his lost notes! Much time had passed since then, years since his quest to locate them with the aid of Hernán: ah, that servant who suddenly disappeared without even bidding him farewell, so ungrateful. The mathematician had attempted to re-elaborate his algebraic lucubrations, without the success he sought, such that the *Mathematical Gazette* rejected his writings. The being at his door uncovered its face. De León y Gama raised the lamp again, he forced open his dull eyes and looked. Policarpo was decrepit. He contemplated him with gravity, not saying a word. Then he covered his face with the shawl and, turning around, he walked away under the torrential rain.

The scientist had assumed the calculist was dead. Once he had seen him appear from out of the shadows and then fade away like the mist, but that was so long ago... What to think? He felt a hint of melancholy and doubt as he wondered if the clockmaker had ever felt meaning in his life. Not all who search will find, he said to himself, tired. He sighed. He had lived long enough not to feel happiness over events like the return of his notes, nor interest in whatever fate they may have suffered. He had abandoned the science of mathematics, and now he put together puzzles that were sent to him from Europe.

He closed his eyes and prayed for the man who was lost under the waters, trudging like a martyr toward an uncertain place.

AS SOON AS SHE SAW THE CALCULATING WHEEL, MARÍA Antonia, the viceroy's wife, thought it would make a fine gift for her daughter. The presents with which she showered her were ostentatious, much like the name she gave her when she came into the world: María Carlota Luisa Guadalupe Carmen Manuela Francisca de Paula Antonia Micaela Lucrecia Josefa Patricia Justa Lorenza Angela y Romana. Although the inventor demanded the machine's return, the Marquis of Branciforte extorted it from his hands: from his fatuous viceroyalty, he was well schooled in the corrupt art of selling public posts, degrees, and royal titles.

María Antonia considered her daughter her only valuable possession. Since her arrival in New Spain, she had fallen into the grips of a tedious somnolence that never left her. Never again. On the journey from Madrid to Cádiz, from Cádiz to America (to the port of Veracruz) and from there to the Capital, she realized that her life in the Old World had vanished forever. Now she was cast off and abandoned, and she yawned constantly as the monotony of life in the New World voided any and all sense of wonder. The frequent visits from bitter old noblewomen repulsed her, but the weight of gold has its price: gold demands life itself in return. Her daughter, on the other hand, filled her with brio: she was the only being in the world able to hang a halo of happiness around her head. The mother hoped the daughter would not grow up to be like her, insipid and ignorant, empty, lacking in vigor and grace, or lose the dignity of her lineage, manifested in the power of an intelligent woman.

Besides, if her daughter were well instructed and learned, this might allow her to return to Europe (the mother would see to this) and conquer the prince of France or of Austria. An educated woman is worth a hundred men, she told her. A product of her ignorance, the poor woman believed the mere possession of the arithmetic machine could imbue whomsoever possessed it with wisdom and knowledge. And so she took great pains to place it in María Carlota's hands, and, when she showed the artefact to the outdated women of her company, she did so boastfully. Look, she exclaimed, this will be Carlota's birthday present.

POLICARPO WANDERED UNDER THE WATER THAT TUMBLED down from the heavens, he trudged across distances flooded by rain and mud. He kept clear of the avenues that already boasted public lighting: lights whose oil was refilled by public employees night after night. The paths he chose were dark and dingy. His soul was in tatters and his body was rigid beneath the feminine garments that hung heavy with the weight of celestial water. Turn by turn, the streets became labyrinths into which he entered, while inclement lightning bolts cut through the night. And so, he advanced down the Street of Saint Inés, the Street of the Love of God, of the Chain, of Flies, of the Monster, of Saint Juanico, until he emerged in the plaza of Saint Sebastián while the storm lashed the stone ground. He remained in the plaza for an hour, as if absorbed in prayer, until the rain began to diminish. De Salazar regained his mobility and began to walk again under the black clouds. There was a curfew that night. He read the names of each avenue as if walking them for the first time. He crossed the bridge beside the plaza and reached the Street of the Mooresses, from there he went back by the Street of the Tombs of Saint Domingo until he reached the Street of the Canoe. The rain was reduced to a faint drizzle, like a murmur of night and falling water, transformed into a rain of luminescent stars: so appeared the water under the light of the lamps hanging from their wooden posts and walls. Drops of light fell and then flowed like a silver-plated stream down the stone street. The rain was so weak that it could not hide the sounds of the night: the song of the crickets and the solitary rhythm of his feet. Policarpo's steps clicked against the wet ground, sharply. Another lightning bolt cracked across the heights, a heavenly gasp to evoke the distance and the depth of anguish. He was followed by the silence of his soul. De Salazar sank into the caverns of his being, he carried on walking, submerged, lost in himself before the curtain of the night, sometimes torn by the lamps. Suddenly he heard a voice: Could you tell me the time?

Again, a lightning bolt plowed through the gloom and illuminated a silhouette dressed in black, its face covered. Policarpo started from his lethargy and looked at the immobile figure of the individual. He had left the clock he sometimes carried with him in his room. That was all he remembered before he noticed that the man was hiding something in his clothes. Silence. Then the glint of a metal blade. Suddenly he knew that before him stood the man sought by the city's lawmen, his peer in the wave of crime and blood, the much feared cutter of throats. Confusion fell from nowhere. The other expected a potential victim, he predicted the softness of a tender lamb's meat. He pulled out his sharpened blade. With a sudden movement, Policarpo uncovered his face and threw his housemaid's shawl to the ground, showing his features eaten away by leprosy. The man with the knife retreated, frightened by this horrible visage; he was about to flee, but he caught his breath and stood on guard with his lethal weapon between his fingers. With murderous instinct, De Salazar crouched as well and extended his arms: his gnarled and heavy hands were ready to grip, their fingers tense and alert. The cutter of throats had also come to understand a blinding truth: he had found the strangler who had brought about the viceregal promise of punishment and torture. Each recognized the other. Policarpo clicked his tongue. The rain picked up again as more lightning crashed and a cold wind whistled, sinister.

Chaos had brought them face to face. The two monsters. The man in black held up a long, sharp knife, his movements agile. Policarpo relied on the powerful and skilled tongs of his hands, his fearsome face, the look of death and his muffled voice of menace: You will find out the time for yourself.

In the works was a violent scene that none would ever witness. The city of Mexico lay asleep under the rain. The monstrous struggle that was there unleashed was the sign of cruel times, perhaps a symbol. Crossed causes and fates, destinies, interrupted silence. With no intention of accepting defeat, both dodged blows and attacks. The two most feared and wanted men in New Spain dove into a portentous confrontation. They measured their distances as they stalked and bellowed. Focused, Policarpo shifted his arms, giving his enemy pause. He fixed his eyes upon him. The cutter of throats, with his weapon in hand, smiled with the insolence of a cunning wolf. He thrust his knife at the chest, again at the face, and again at the neck of his adversary: all missed their mark. At once, with his weapon he evaded the fingers that avidly sought to administer their fatal pressure. Then another uncertain thrust that seemed to meet something. The man in black laughed, then he felt his throat contract. The murderous, well-aimed fingers had trapped his neck, they grasped him with disproportionate strength. Both men stumbled and fell gasping to the ground. Their bodies rolled in battle, one struggling to free himself and the other to keep his grip. The water fell without fail, the only sound was the din of the new storm born of the rain. Much time had passed since the skies last overflowed in such a way; they insisted upon offering a sign. The knife lay on the ground. The bodies twisted in a titanic struggle, in which the night's sentence had already decided the name of the man who would die on that street. The knife-wielder's body began to give in, moment by moment he lost his strength. Policarpo stood, panting, and looked down at the motionless man, his face still covered. He left him there, not even thinking of pulling aside the anonymous killer's veil. His work was not yet done, and he was in haste to finish it. He had planned it as he wandered the avenues.

He felt a scratch on his side, his only wound from the fight. And, without another thought, he walked straight to the residence of the viceroy. 卐

PROLEPSIS
Axiom

Mankind is a business that has time, necessity, and fortune working against it, as well as the stupid and ever growing primacy of the number.

MARGUERITE YOURCENAR

I met Marino at a conference on mathematical logic and algorithms they put on in the Department. Amanda, my wife, had quarreled with me before leaving home, never to return. After this incomprehensible abandonment, which plunged me into a state of deep depression (about twenty-five days ago), Leticia, a friend, invited me to the conference that, she claimed, would surely stimulate my mind and lighten the load on my spirit. *Marino Montero: Elements of Mathematical Logic based on Modular Arithmetic*, read the poster for the talk. I accepted her invitation, intrigued by the suggestive title. My first impression of him (as a professor recently invited to the Department) was that of a brilliant, daring, audacious individual. He immediately had a profound effect on me. But if there is anything we should heed in human relationships it is not the first but the second impression that every individual leaves on those with whom they interact. the second impression determines whether the light touch of their presence might one day secure a lasting friendship, or if it will remain as is, a plain and simple exchange. Marino needed no second impressions. A conversation with him made it clear that he was not only brilliant, he was someone exceptional, unique. I immediately tried to curry his favor, confident that he was one of those chosen few whose blessing, whose minimal admiration, we all so desperately desire.

To speak of the man is to build him out of ideas, out of the rain of dreams left behind after his death. It is also to dredge up his problems and his doubts. The world has problems, almost all the ones that seem irresolvable tend not to be, and among them are the problems of living space and survival, not to mention others similar, or those that cause a man and a woman who have loved one another to drift apart due to matters of surprising triviality (it was thirty-two days since my separation from Amanda). Most irresolvable dilemmas are not found in the world of matter: we find them in the world of ideas. They are questions of the intellect, important for individuals who think too much and who sink into profound abstractions from which some never return. Among these solutionless problems, there is one of particular importance in mathematics, not only due to its technical difficulty but also due to its wide-ranging implications in the philosophy of knowledge: such problems torture brilliant, uneasy minds like Marino's. The challenge was proposed by a Dutch mathematician who emerged from the darkness in 1910, a year of upheaval and revolutions in the world: L.E.J. Brouwer. Brouwer tells us it is impossible to ascertain the truth or falsehood of a sentence like the following: *In the decimal expression of π there exist a hundred consecutive zeros.* The problem is serious, as it refers not only to this already enigmatic number, but to any other irrational number as well, and it might refer not to one hundred zeros, but to a greater or lesser quantity. In any case, one cannot be sure if they exist or not; in order to do so, we would need to expand the decimals to infinite digits. And so, we remain in the dark. This is a problem that reveals the non-universal nature of the law of excluded middle. In mathematics, there are questions without answers. The principle of excluded middle is an Aristotelic law according to which, for a given proposition, there exist only two possibilities of truth: if a proposition *p* is true, the negation of *p*, *not p*, is false.

Brouwer's problem is not only a problem of logic: it is a problem of the infinite.

In the Department, I learned quickly that there are things one ought not take lightly. One of them is the infinite.

Legend tells us the last human being to dominate the mathematical spectrum in its entirety was H. Poincaré, the father of topology. When I met Marino, I started to doubt that this was true: his research took in countless subjects and was published in mathematical journals of global prestige. I pored over them with dedication, prisoner to a mix of admiration and envy. If only I could have come up with even one of his formulations…, I moaned to Leticia. His demonstrations of theorems, reflections, and conjectures seemed to orbit the whole mathematical world. *The American Mathematical Monthly*, *The Mathematical Gazette*, *Epsilon*, and many other journals published his contributions.

My first *misunderstanding* with Marino was the result of an essay I sent to be published in the Department's newsletter. In some small way, I thought it might upset his particular sensibilities. And so I got to know him, gaining that *second impression* of which I was speaking. In the essay, I laid out a few concepts—intelligent, in my judgment—regarding contemporary mathematics. I will cite an excerpt from the piece and, to clarify the reasons behind what happened next, I will place the phrases that set off the story in italics:

> *Eternal Debate*
> Some, even in the days of Virtual Reality, argue as to whether or not Mathematics, more than a science, is a form of language. Is it created? Is it discovered? All we know is that no one knows the answer. Perhaps it is not so daring to define

mathematics as a formal art. *He who affirms that Mathematics is incompatible with reality and situates it exclusively in the world of ideas denies it, and not only does he deny Mathematics, but also history and the future itself, because the historic process of the world is the long-standing process of Mathematics.* It has already been shown that an axiomatic system is not necessarily self-sufficient, in the sense that any affirmation related to its subject might be proven only with the axioms of said system. The complexity of any issue lying at the borders of such a system makes the demonstrations it requires ever more difficult. In Mathematics, everything must be demonstrated, and nonetheless we find heretical mathematicians who foretell the death of mathematical demonstration. There are others who accept the idea of some machine that might carry out the task. Discourse on the future of mathematics has been treated with indifference; most futurists avoid the subject.

Mathematics, or rather the set of all possible mathematics, did not emerge when man acquired the capacity to make the number abstract. It emerged when he understood the recurrence of certain phenomena, when he could be sure that day followed night, night followed day, day followed night, and so on. When the human being knew once and for all that it was possible to find an order in the world, a harmony that connects its objects. Mathematics was born from this finding. *The number came later.*

A few days after the publication of *Eternal Debate*, Marino stood before me with a copy of the newsletter, which he threw down on the table where I sat drinking coffee. Some say mathematicians are machines that turn coffee into theorems. Nothing could be further from the truth: some drink coffee to forget. It was no wonder because, I must admit, the essay was written with the intention of sparking a reaction from Marino. Looking at me with that dry seriousness of his, Marino interrupted my calculations. Your pretentious little piece doesn't convince me, he snapped. I snuck a look at the title I had devised. Marino, I responded, all the texts are revised by competent people. My publication passed the peer review, and two of the reviewers suggested changes and clarifications. Those idiots don't know anything either, he proceeded, they think they have a brain just because they have a doctorate. As for you, he added, I almost thought you were a little more intelligent. And he finished off: You've let me down with such stupidity...

That *you've let me down*, coming out of his mouth, sounded like a final disqualification. Even if I wanted to, I couldn't take it as a simple reproach, it was something *else* that, from that day on, made me lose sleep. When I saw him in the hallway, I became tense and nervous. In seminars, I tried to get his attention, making eloquent comments and asking engaging questions of the speakers, hoping uselessly that the weight of his eyes would rest on me.

Marino was one of those people who deeply hate mediocrity. He couldn't settle for isolated results in any area of mathematics. He created complete theories.

One afternoon, in the Department café, he and Carolina sat down next to my table. The young woman was one of Marino's many girlfriends, and Amanda had introduced her to me a year before. In fact, *she was a lot like Amanda*, not physically, but due to the gestures she often made, the movements of her body. Even the types of clothes they wore had much in common, the other members of the Department had commented on it. For his part, if Marino needed anything else to boast about, it was his skill with women.

Carolina had beautiful features and, above all, a laugh that was somewhere between childish and flirtatious (that was one difference from Amanda), which could often be disturbing, even more if one looked into her deep, light eyes. But she looked at no one with them, no one but Marino... On her long, tanned legs, which boldly showed below her miniskirt, there rested a laptop that, she said, was a birthday present from her mother. She shot Marino a complicitous look. Then she turned on the machine. Marino settled into his seat and closed his eyes. He asked her to come up with an arithmetic operation, any one that came to her mind. Amused, she threw out figures, suggesting divisions and multiplications between them, and he responded. On the computer screen, the results were proven. I began to understand the game. My hands held up a book published by the prestigious Springer Verlag, which cited one of Marino's articles on modular forms. While watching the expressions of excitement on Carolina's face, I tried to concentrate on my reading. Then, as if suddenly noticing my existence, Marino turned and waved his hand at me. The look on his face said *you might just surprise me*, and he invited me to participate in the game. I gave him two whole numbers of considerable magnitude (how could I forget them, one was a multiple of fifty-five, the number of days my wife and I had been separated), and I asked him for the product. Marino had the answer before his girlfriend's fingers had finished typing in the numbers. And he was right. And so we remained for a while, I spitting out numbers and operations, he using his head and responding, even with square roots and differing orders of magnitude.

Marino was one of those people whom some magazines call an *idiot savant*, without the qualifier of *idiot*, of course. Sometimes these *savants* appear in films or television programs, showing off their numerical skills. In other activities, such beings are often inept, even mentally retarded. We might bump into them on the streets or in the metro, not noticing that they are counting multitudes of people with a single gaze, and carrying out complicated mental calculations in mere seconds. I felt encumbered, used. The number is primordial, and it was what it is before the emergence of Man, Marino assured me with an unknowable shimmer in his eyes.

I sensed it would be best for me to avoid him.

Marino had, nonetheless, two notable defects: one physical and the other psychological: the first was a case of allergic asthma brought on by flowers, the winter cold, and stress: he was skilled enough to ensure that no one noticed it. In a certain debate with another scholar regarding the validity or invalidity of a possible definition of sets, bewildered by the other man's foolishness, those of us who witnessed the discussion up close noticed a slight difficulty in Marino's breathing. His other deficiency was his absolute refusal to accept the existence of the number zero, a risible trait in someone like him. He wrote a million, for example, in exponential notation or even with letters to avoid the repulsion of marking down zeros, of watching them appear like intimidating enemies before him. For this reason, the Brouwer question troubled him. He was allergic to the zero.

Days later, I saw him again in the café, this time by accident. He was alone, and he was indeed transforming coffee into theorems. I pretended not to have seen him, but when he left, I noticed that he had forgotten a book on the table. I picked it up before someone else could claim it. My curiosity was killing me. It was a copy of the *Scottish Book*, the mythical collection of mathematical problems proposed, among others, by the great Ulam. It always surprised me to read that the *Scottish Book* was buried under a dry soccer field while its authors, scattered across Europe and the United States, tried to survive the Second World War, under the solemn promise that the survivors would return to dig it up. On the dust cover, Marino had noted down (a few lines by T.S. Eliot):

And even the Abstract Entities
Circumambulate her charm;
But our lot crawls between dry ribs
To keep our metaphysics warm.

The number in its infinite primacy. The Pythagorean dictum, *all is number*, made me question the power of words. It has always pained me to know that I am not only, as if in some dystopian future, a single number, but rather many numbers that classify my person on a certificate, on a card, on a driver's license, on my voter ID, on my checkbook, on my professional credentials, on my medical records... Every one of these documents is dealt with by the corresponding functionary in terms of numbers: on each one, my name is lost. Who could have imagined that the Greek mysticism of the number would become the purist cult of Number Theorists, and then the zeal for the creation of cryptographic code, which protects the databases that give access to stratospheric bank accounts, like those of corrupt politicians who make money by bleeding their people dry. The number against the name. The money number. The dissolution of the individual in a sea of figures, of the population census, the census of poverty and malnourishment, the census of war and death.

Among others, among the golden number, the real number, the complex number, the hypercomplex number, the p-adic number, or the transfinite number, a special type of number stands out that can determine the measure of chaos: special exponents resulting from a dynamic of the modelable world. I wonder if a number exists that might determine the magnitude of evil, of hate, of suffering. Or a number that quantifies the pain of a broken heart. When I learned to count, numbers amazed me. I was innocent then.

I wasn't sure whether to return the book to Marino or keep it. I didn't want to see him again and let him humiliate me. In spite of my reluctance, I decided to find him and give him back his property. I arrived at his office door, which was already half open. If I had knocked to get his attention, several of the events I will presently describe would not have taken place. I opened the door slowly, I only wanted to give him the book and then get out of there, losing myself in the hallways leading to the Department's botanical garden. As I cast my eyes over the spot where I suspected Marino would be sitting, they fell upon an empty seat. However, to the left side, near the entrance, I noticed something that left me frozen in place: Marino was standing with his back turned to the lateral wall of the door, in front of a computer. The machine was performing arithmetic calculations. At first, I detected in his stance a sense of irony, perhaps of humor: it was as if he were prostate before the machine, as if worshipping it. Someone as brilliant as he! It was contradictory, ridiculous. The vision brought to mind pagan apostasies of forgotten times, nameless cults disappeared from humanity due to their obscenity. At one conference, Marino had stated, among colleagues and students, that the machine was the mediator between man and abstract objects, even between the numbers of the world of ideas. There are numbers that cannot even be imagined, he declared suggestively, but which can still be accessed through the computer, or the calculator, whatever you want to call it. There are unnameable figures, of orders beyond the scope of words.

My mistrust was growing. I tried to push what I had seen out of my mind, without success. Behind my eyelids, the image of the office persisted. By the time I noticed, I was making myself sick over it. But we also tend to spy on that which shocks and fascinates us, we follow it down intricate paths sown with danger. At risk of losing my position, I found a way, night after night, to get into his office and find whatever I could, anything to find out who he was. And so I came across the notebook in which, besides his mathematical advances, he wrote down his introspections, all his poisons. It was not a diary nor anything like it.

> *Note from Marino:* The number is cold and severe. The number does not lie. In dreams I have seen a new arithmetic in which the zero does not exist.

In informal conversations, Marino stood up for those mathematicians who undertook their research within the realm of the abstract, searching for Divinity. Perhaps, he said, what they proposed was a Religion of the Mind. After assuring us that he was not joking, he went on to explain that cults had been a part of human life since time immemorial. And, seconding Galileo, he stated that mathematics is the search for the Mind of God.

In a certain period of the history of Japan, peasants offered their gods geometrical theorems on thin tablets of wood: *sangaku*. The samurai too, between 1700 and 1800, after practicing *bushido* and sharpening their katanas, would retire to their rooms to carve the solutions to mathematical problems, then offering their *sangaku* in Shinto or Buddhist temples to gods who liked math.

The Religion of the Mind is something similar, Marino opined. It granted the idea of a Platonic world, full of the purity of silence and the silence of purity. The mind, he continued, is a mechanism used to access the place in which all is Mind. *There*, the mathematical world exists for itself, waiting for us to discover its entities. There is God.

> *Note from Marino:* I seek a form of science and aesthetics in which coldness reins. I have arrived at concepts, exclusively numerical, that would explain the reasons for the existence of the spheres. Starting from the hypersphere, I have found the *artificial numbers.*

Artificial numbers, how could I understand that? I accept that my mind is barely strong enough to understand the abstract structure that makes up the natural numbers. Number Theory studies natural numbers: our first contact with the countable. In contrast, this maniacal researcher had discovered his own numbers, which were generated out of a homomorphism of action over products of prime entities, making them coincide with particular points on the surface of multidimensional spheres.

Sometimes Marino praised chance, the unpredictable beauty of chance. He made bets in the casinos of Avenida de los Insurgentes, so controversial to some. I remember how he described with fascination the movement of the dice after they were thrown, those strange cubes obedient to the numbers of uncertainty.

After I counted up the days that separated me from my wife's departure (ninety-eight), Leticia said to me: Don't give in to the tyranny of numbers, you'll be even unhappier. But what are numbers without tyranny? Unless, speaking in general terms, the abstract world from which they come, as Marino would maintain, is also a kingdom of lonely coldness. I had never paused to think deeply about the subject. The *Abstract Entities*... It is a matter of arduous planning. The Platonic inheritance of a world of ideas, independent of man, in which perfect concepts exist, was attractive to past theologians. Besides, there is a long tradition of interaction between Christian theology and Platonic philosophy. Saint Augustine hesitated nervously upon relating the omnipotence of God to the truths resident in the world of perfect ideas. In systematic thought, there is a problem: certain principles of logic and arithmetic seem to be irrevocable, and for this reason they place certain restrictions upon the free action of God.

The mathematicians of the past believed in the existence of the Divine Mind, in which perfection lived. Others, more contemporary, have a special attitude toward mathematical structures (which, to them, are permanent and immutable). At the University of Geneva, mathematician Paul Bernins declared that mathematical objects are *deprived of any link to the reflexive subject*; in other words, they are isolated from the personal influence of the mathematician. Kurt Gödel, a revolutionary of modern mathematics, was also an exponent of Platonism, and he upheld a surprising adherence to the idea of the objective reality of entities, which is the everyday preoccupation of any logician. Then there's Ramanujan, the young autodidact: *I believe mathematical reality resides outside of us and it is our function to rediscover and observe it... 317 (for example) is a prime number* not *because we create it so, nor because our minds are conformed in one direction more than another, but because* it is so, *as mathematical reality is built this way.* Sir Roger Penrose, a multifaceted English genius, supports this stance and assures of the existence of geometrical configurations that man, assisted by the machine, discovers (fractal complexes, for example) and that *are not an invention of the human mind: these structures are already* there, *they are discovered as Everest is discovered.*

I started to experience confusion and fever, insomnia. How real could the world of symbols be? When I fell asleep, I had nightmares in which Marino sometimes appeared. I was running after him, hoping to take from him a key, or a code, to these worlds of infinite purity. In other dreams, I was trapped in the world of the *Abstract Entities*, from which I could not return.

I saw him a couple more times, performing his mental calculations, his face tense and his forehead sweaty, concentrating as if possessed. He was making tremendous effort in this *game of resistance*, computing all the decimal places of some irrational number allowed into his mind. He ended up exhausted, like a flacid automaton. He went pale, and his voice was stifled. When I looked at him, I felt something that I couldn't quite name, but that I somehow associated with fear.

Instructions for the learned (note from Marino):

Instructions for Archimedes:
Count grains of sand and dust. Calculate and count until you die. Then, from the bottom of the well, pronounce the number. Divide the form of death into a thousand pieces and every piece into a thousand pieces to uncover its secrets to me. Light the dawn of days with your mirror. Bloody your knuckles of the edges of the geometrical body. Invent an endless theorem that leads to madness.

Instructions for Galileo:
While Simplicio falls from the Tower, observe that Salviati's dagger is hidden under his garments, eager to jab and to wound. Without the Tower's leaning, the shadow disappears at midday. Do you see the pendulum swinging? In that synchronicity, the swaying of your sentence is announced (men move too). Accept the pyre's flames without fear.

Instructions for A. Einstein:
Mind the black hole that lies in wait for you, not even light escapes its abyss. Do not stop attending to the equation that twists up from the line and screams out the truth you never hear. Wind the clock. Watch the compass and repeat the mental photon experiment. Show me that gravity exists. Dive into the preying center of the black hole because God will never leave the dice game.

One night as I furtively leafed through Marino's notebook, I noticed there were new additions. One of them called my attention. The note said: The *Entities* deserve more than the offering of a single mind. Then: I have thrown the dice and six fell after three: suddenly the deep sleep of reason came.

This man's mind is off-key, I thought, surely he is plotting something. It's not the case that bad-faith ideas were sprouting from my mind out of jealousy at his genius: what touched my nerve was that a copy of *Reforma* from two days prior was lying on his desk, and its pages caught my attention. The headline mentioned nine deaths. Take note: Marino had thrown the dice. Six and three, in first module arithmetic, make nine. I don't know, I suppose I should have given notice to the authorities, although it is well known that the Mexican police do not act until they see bodies. I feared I would find myself face to face with this insane genius, and that he would discover me going through his things. I stayed out of the Department for two weeks.

I walked lost and confused through the city. I aimlessly stepped on and off the metro. On every face that moved past, I saw Marino. I ate little in those days, any food I consumed made me nauseous. What was I thinking? I would turn on the television just to turn it off as soon as it winked its electronic eye. I sank into the web of information: the virtual highway offered itself up to me on the luminous screen, while my fingers typed like mad. I navigated across seven seas of information bytes, more information everywhere, unwanted information that I bumped into as if it had me surrounded. Like what I read and reread at this very moment:

The origin of numbers

Numbers are coagulations of the waves of symmetry, they are the memory of symmetry and memory itself is a mirror or a duplicator. Numbers are an expression of the natural world, which, to build its work, is based on regularities. Said symmetry is also cerebral, it is physical (electromagnetic waves or subatomic particles). It is cosmological (the earth's rotation, light and shadow), physiological, idiomatic, and graphic (the shape of letters, the tone of speech, breath). It is temporal since time is duplicable. (If a clock is reflected in a mirror with three lobes and two valleys, this duplicates the image. So, while the hour hand of the physical clock makes a complete turn, the same hand on the reflected clock makes two)... And light... If you take a photo of a photo, in front of the mirror, when the light is reflected, the light bounces back and comes out of the mirror, such that in the photo you see the flash and a circular ray of light, perfect and dynamic, that comes and goes, that starts and ends in the mirror but is developed outside... (take it with the light of day). Since the ray is white, within the photo there remains a small rainbow... The very subatomic particles, whether they are called particles or forces or relations or functions within the cords, have their perfect duplicates in antiparticles (the mirror's reflection). Memory, mirror, symmetry, and number are functional, natural synonyms... Right and left chirality dictate that there are axes (*01*, *10*), they are palindromic bus tickets when they still came on numbered paper: *18481*. The four is the axis, but even without the four (*1881*) there is still an axis. We are speaking of supersymmetries, since simple symmetry is found in any number (*5*) because it signifies repetition, either of a unit or a piece. To be matter, it must be reflected toward both sides of an axis, and this gives rise to symmetry... So the number represents the symmetrical axis of nature and, therefore, the intermediate state, and can be defined as the human face of visible or invisible symmetries because they erase all of the likely spectrum of what there is... Its magic consists of erasing even the unknown. (We might not know a star, but it still allows us to determine at what distance it glows).

To add is the action of describing unfolding symmetries:

$1 = {}^{*}$

$2 = {}^{**}$ unfolding or repetition of the previous movement (symmetry)

$3 = {}^{***}$ the same.

We are able to add because we have memory, which is a copying mirror. Adding and adding and naming the movement, symmetry and the like... Unfolding and repeating a movement, again and again. Definition of symmetry? Similitude, reflection, similar movement. What comes first, the chicken or the egg? The mirror (or, rather, the action of reflecting and duplicating) is anterior to the number.

It was signed by a certain Hugo Luchetti, who finally wondered: *Where am I standing when I understand?*

On the nightly TV news, they repeated the report on those strange deaths that were mentioned in the paper in Marino's office: in a room in an apartment in Colonia Tránsito they found nine bodies, lying in formation in a hallway. The news anchors emphasized the criminal's *inhumanity*. For their part, the papers speculated about the motive of the murder, attributing it to organized crime. In a heated discussion, the district attorney rejected the opinion of a forensic investigator who suggested suicide. The autopsy, after all, turned up residue of powerful sleep-inducing drugs like Loramet and Rohypnol in their stomachs. Anyone might have suspected a mass suicide. But there was another detail: all nine were tied up with resistant nylon: they could not have taken their own lives. Nonetheless, as the attorney insisted again, organized crime behaves differently, they deliver the coup de grâce in the back of the neck, that is their *norm* and these facts do not back it up.

In my own notebook, which I carried during those taxing days (a sham, a meager copy of Marino's), in search of any element that might lend clarity to my story, I found this:

> Two weeks outside the Department, far from my research. Nothing to do. Walking through the streets and returning home, alone, with my books and paradoxes, in this nightmare. Today it has been one hundred twenty days since, citing my excessive dedication to mathematics, Amanda left for another man's apartment. I do not miss this ghost, I have learned to be apart from her warmth (false, it is the negation of the previous proposition that boasts truth value). One hundred twenty days! I am still passing through the phases of mourning... I go online in search of an article on differential equations and I end up stumbling across offers to subscribe to forums, with ads for whores offering their bodies, with ads of all kinds, or pages for bestiality, zoophilia, necrophilia, lesbianism, sadism, others for pornography in cartoon form... I should avoid all this chaos of information and head straight

for what I am looking for but not finding. Out of inertia, I type meaningless phrases about the possible and the impossible, dates, names, places. I research technological, scientific, mathematical breakthroughs, and I sink again into another submarine current of data.

This is how I came across a number that is remarkable among all numbers. I call it *the number*.

When I got back to the Department, things lolled in a healthy normality. No nightmare, just life. No delusions. The gardens seemed greener and the people more enthused. The first familiar face I saw was Amanda's, or I imagined as much after the first glance, but in reality it was Carolina's. I shivered when, this time, she saw fit to look at me with her light eyes before greeting me cheerfully. The weather was cloudy and pleasant, and I was feeling well, until far away, crossing the walkway that connects the library to the cafe, I saw Marino.

I had to wait until nighttime before sneaking into Marino's office. The batteries in my flashlight were almost dead: I had little time to scour through everything I could. Marino had moved things from their places, the bookshelf, the coffee pot, the computer, the sticky notes. The desk was new and the drawers were locked. I didn't see the notebook anywhere, and my flashlight began to blink. The notes must have been under lock and key in the desk. I left before the light could go out.

The *number*, in italics to distinguish it from all others, is strange in essence. It can only be reached by manipulating a specific advanced algorithm with the aid of a computer: a complex Wolfram algorithm. It is an *Abstract Entity* that was not invented by man, but discovered. When I observe it, I can hardly accept that such a number exists. I have played with it until noticing that it can be reached by arithmetically manipulating the positive root of a quadratic equation, an algebraic formula that is simple and disconcerting all at once: the formula I write in ink here: $x^2 - 3^3x + 3^3 = 0$. I doubt anyone else has noticed the importance of such an insignificant equation.

I returned to Marino's office with new batteries in my flashlight. For the locks on the drawers, it was not difficult to find some Korean-made lockpicks.

There were the notes. As I expected, I found something new:

> *Axiom*
> An axiom is something that is accepted as true from the start, to give way to something more complex. I have found no axiom that man has accepted without question since the beginning of time besides this: All men are mortal.

Reading on, I found this:

> *Dialectic of the dice*
> There is nothing simpler, yet nothing more beautiful, to emulate chance than a pair of dice. They give their bearer the certainty of carrying chance in his pocket. The dice game is more interesting if they are thrown one by one. Double chance, double surprise. Each die must be medium-sized, not too small so as not to get lost, nor too big so as not to show off, and dice made of elephant or walrus ivory are preferable, as they have a pleasant weight in their pouch or in the hands before they are thrown, since when they are shaken they produce a special, powerful sound. The dots must be burned on

with a white-hot iron, thus they will never be erased from the touch of a sweaty hand. The twelve faces of each die are like the twelve columns of the sacred temples the prophets saw in dreams. In the world of ideas, the shining temples must be so. The *Abstract Entities*, which wander through them in their cold beauty, still appear to me in dreams. They are so real. I always touch them. I am convinced that I must take them more seriously.

Marino. Marino. When did I first notice that you and I are alike?

Note from Marino: Soon, I will throw the dice again.

In 1966, European students held in their hands the first edition of the *Course in General Mathematics* by C. Pisot and Zamansky, based on which, in order to fortify their mathematical skills, G. Lefort composed a difficult problem set for the same students. Little is known of the authors of the *Course*, especially the first, Pisot, about whom many curious scholars have inquired (intrigued upon seeing a reference to him in the Virtual Space of *Mathematica©*). We can imagine him walking through the hallways of a university in his native France, with his bitter coffee in a chalk-dusted hand, a book of higher arithmetic or algebra and a copy of *Le Monde* under his arm. A ghostlike figure who wanders through the mind of a small group of number-lovers, who dozes in the pages of high-minded arithmetic research, who floats on cyberspace that can barely touch him with its virtual geometry, or, perhaps, who resides in the world of ideas. Born in 1910, the same year when the Dutch mathematician Luitzen E.J. Brouwer formulated his famous insolubility problem—the problem of the excluded third—Pisot shared the numerical obsession of Ramanujan, Hardy, Dedekind, and Cantor, especially regarding algebraic numbers, which he researched widely. He must also have familiarized himself with the intuitionist theses of Mathematics proposed by Brouwer himself. I have asked about Pisot with the same curiosity, and little is known. I like to think of him in a world full of activity, of interminable discussions with colleagues until the late hours of the night, with the blackboard full of symbols and abstractions. Sometimes I think of him alone, meditating on his theorems, writing them out in careful detail. It's as if I can see him sitting at his desk, demanding silence while he swiftly jots down his ideas on paper so as not to lose them, later getting up for another coffee and returning to his desk to leaf through *Le Monde*, reading the news of the day, perhaps blurting out a *merde* upon seeing reports on the stock market or the repression of the world's student movements. I wonder if Pisot was right- or left-handed, if he was well-liked in the university, if he sympathized with communism or capitalism, or if, at the time, he protested against the use of the atomic bomb in the Second World War. What must he have thought of the Allies?

I try to continue reconstructing his life in my thoughts. I also dive into the Internet, but I don't find much. From his work, I select: *La répartition modulo 1 et les nombres algébriques (Annali della Scuola Norm. Sup. Pisa, Ser. 2, 7 (1938), 205-248)*. On his life: *Charles Pisot, France, (1910—1984)*.

Under various pretexts, like requesting explanations of the axioms of Zermelo Fraenkel or asking for help holding her books while she checked if her car keys were in her pocket, Carolina started spending more time around me. Ergo, the reason behind her smile upon my return to the Department was explained. Possibly, I thought, she is looking for a substitute for Marino, just as I, without fully accepting it, sought a substitute for Amanda. For this reason, when she first rested her hand, as if carelessly, on my own, I furtively pulled mine away. The temptation was intense, but I avoided it every time with unrealistic excuses. I didn't want Marino to see us and misunderstand the circumstances. Days later, nonetheless, I took Carolina by the hand to help her jump over a puddle on the Department's terrace. After that, I allowed her to hold on. The texture of her skin hurt me, because it wasn't Carolina touching me, but rather the Amanda who had abandoned me a hundred thirty-one days before. The Amanda who had known me just as I was, just as I had known her. The woman I had loved and hated, but loved much more. You're not Amanda, I said aloud, and Carolina laughed when she heard. She laughed in the way women laugh when they begin to distill the venom of seduction. I was afraid, and I decided to pull away from her before we were seen. But Marino saw us.

The last night I went through Marino's things, I read in his notes:

> *Six plus three module one*
> I have given in to my mind's insistence on making things clear. Any other way, this work would not be complete, and if someone in the future were to read it, he would understand nothing of my marvellous passage through the labyrinth of life. After I threw the dice some days ago and saw with pleasure how each number appeared, I knew what I would do. Six plus three is nine...

I stopped reading. The truth came to me in a flash. It had to be the nine tragic events in the news. With the *deep dream of reason*, he had referred to the death caused by the sleeping pills. What was I doing there in the cage of this madman, this murderer? I was overwhelmed and the world briefly faded to black as the notes fell from my hands. The notebook lay open, close to the last full page, among whose chaos was a photo of Carolina. Pages later, I read:

Axiom: He is mortal.

I don't believe his *He* referred to all humans, or to Socrates, or to the divine. I left Mexico City. My previous fear was nothing compared to what I felt now. I was running for my life. If I had taken the notes, I believe they would have served as good evidence to have him arrested as a suspect for the nine deaths (or for planning more?), but I left them in their place, intact, anticipating any possible incident. My hands were empty and my life hung from a thread. I had nowhere to go. And how could I keep other citizens from falling into danger? I boarded a bus for Puebla, a familiar place to me, as I had lived there for a time while conducting research.

After a light sleep on the bus, passing by San Martín Texmelucan with the icy volcanic peaks of Popocatépetl and Iztaccíhuatl as the background, not only of the sown fields but also of my nightmare, I flicked through the printed pages of my numerical findings. There was no way around it, the *number* was irrational.

Puebla was Marino's native city, and the only place I knew besides Mexico City. I sought refuge there for a few days in the small apartment of a graduate student who was attending a conference. I still don't understand how it occurred to me to inquire into Marino Montero's past. I searched in the phone book for names of people who might be related to him. There was no one. In vain, I leafed through the pages of archived newspapers. To no avail, I asked after him at the local universities where he might have passed through before leaving for his doctorate at MIT. Until I had an idea. He must have been exceptional since his infancy, I thought, surely they didn't send him to a public school. One by one, I checked the private schools until, almost ready to accept defeat, I came across a prestigious German school. At my behest, they pulled his file from their old records: Let's see, based on what you're looking for, there are a few that might match. The names never matched. Looking over the records again, the director (an old lady of around seventy) admitted she did not remember him, but she was sure at least three students skilled at the art of mental calculation had passed through her classrooms. The engineer Martínez, one of their professors, according to the director's tired memory, was a wonderful person who died in a premature and inexplicable fashion. He did not deserve to die like that, the woman told me, it seems they pushed him off the staircase as he walked down, we never knew exactly how it happened because it appeared to be an accident, but I never bought that story. I don't know why, the old lady added, but I have always had the impression that one of those young geniuses had something to do with it, and I don't think it was a coincidence that the family of the most brilliant of them moved shortly after, taking the young man to Mexico City. Look, I can tell you from experience that these super-gifted children tend to be troubled people, not to mention arrogant and jealous, and they always challenge their professors. He may have contended with one such child. The old woman's face wore an expression of weariness, contained by the years. Before leaving, I asked which class Professor Martínez had taught to the alleged offender. Mathematics, she answered.

A few weeks later, I returned to Mexico City in a burst of valor. I investigated the apartment where the nine victims had appeared. I was told that months before it had been rented by someone who claimed to live in Los Angeles, who would only come sporadically on business. (Los Angeles, California? I'm sure, since Marino is from Puebla, he could easily extrapolate names, play with words, with the celestial allusion to the origin of his *Puebla de los Ángeles*). The doorman mentioned that the *foreigner* sometimes had guests. Yes! I said to myself, I need search no longer: it's *him*. How many other deaths had he caused? How many more?

Out of curiosity, and in case it might add something to my search through the city of Puebla, I was able to find the old newspapers that told of the death of Professor Martínez. There I found something of which the director of Marino's old school was perhaps unaware: a police investigator interested in Martínez's case abruptly committed suicide. His family knew of no precedent of suicidal tendencies. It caught my attention that Colonel Ibáñez of the District Attorney's office, who had recently been engaged in the investigation of the nine deaths in the Mexico City apartment, had also died. His passing was the result of a butane gas leak: the volatile substance was set alight when the policeman struck a light after walking into his house with his family. They all died.

The sooner I acted the better.

Had I put my mind to it, I could easily have convinced the police to investigate my suspicions of Marino: they would have listened to the director of the German school, with all her memories and uncertainties. The foreman of the building in Colonia Tránsito would have had no problem recognizing a real picture of Marino, in conjunction with the spoken picture he had helped me put together. But if I had anything in common with Marino, even if he considered me a pusillanimous and gray subject, it was the fact that I also liked to see things brought to their end.

Yes, it was difficult for Marino to assimilate the zero. He suffered a phobia of the figure, and perhaps a certain horror at its exist-ence. The zero made him feel as if he were standing in the pres-ence of nothing, the void. Who likes the void? When he heard about the Brouwer problem of the many possible or impossible zeros in an irrational number, Marino claimed he was uncon-cerned. Bah! he exclaimed, we would need all those digits to do the research. They are infinite, did you forget? Marino relied on this reasoning regarding the infinite, he took it lightly. But the fact that we cannot predict if there is or isn't a monstrous quantity of contiguous zeros in a number, where there is apparently no rea-son for them to be there, does not mean we cannot find them by sheer luck in some number or another. The zeros could even trick us, making us think the number was rational, especially if we do not take care to consider it closely. I prepared a surprise that the crazed number-lover wasn't going to like. I sent him a message un-der the name of Professor Martínez (*a ghost of your past, remem-ber, Marino?*) giving him the instructions to reach an *interesting* number, through *Mathematica©*, to 5600 decimal places. It was the strange irrational I had found in the sands of the virtual beach, something I was sure would serve as an assault on his conceptions of perfection. Because Marino loved perfection, in his way, and he was too sensitive to such things.

On his screen would appear, in bytes, illuminated by the flow of millions of electrons, a crucial, surprising, monstrous number: one of Pisot's numbers. The *number*.

The next day, Marino was found dead in his office, face down beside his desk. The forensic report declared that he had suffered a sudden asthma attack and was caught without his inhaler. His office was cleared out days later. While Carolina and I removed his belongings so the space could be taken by another visiting professor, I restarted his computer, whose monitor had been frozen since then. Holding me close, Carolina looked down at the lit screen, where several programs still shone open in their windows, including his inbox. I have no reason to think Marino ignored the message from *Martínez*. With a final gaze of stupefaction, and his body surely rigid with fear, his eyes must have been fixed upon the overwhelming figure:

$$\left(\left(\frac{2}{\left(3\left(9+\sqrt{69}\right)\right)}\right)^{1/3} + \frac{\left[\frac{1}{2}\left(9+\sqrt{69}\right)\right]^{1/3}}{3^{2/3}}\right)^{30000} =$$

5.04316596065665493215059469242757481077610274680893503167
8444677128757182264862106103980765819340682753857825408213
30947870035477787176694685987718254576565515786375180040308
41080877201973602630453775992992526007874643437115478340662
6566542422631671379704708764600286765957208825537299414139
91192954257293905515987341623164931728987789298548218169139
5638163536241282159945102531936490365111022151523381436452
79048930913371354240272588991921619868232355282955810598732
00107875550497563219302434498746973208148942951387505081
50895446761509382533298841076293708778366046553068685772
85538664595048264681443930199901657433773640659222556791170
9051797128549077311912778888144108736659703862174018641106
91757499520236594196403021789595612659015207824257477907567
8185904725211878343979501048953268614290340265384740790514
6487735500216875475845252225041904360870681078279227104457
22736236879669324173378416116695919841030467768296491940
90438705230027320037702374804434310323316910942614411443802
98348751920199059562790511888049750265002682883521913896
85849628968612357880766725385147857934444955391441537519

37285121796122315842862423189949212117527981448636085804805
65751208648179069823594655467910333455703061443068891823759
65935558188718231183977511187240921162728629126713811608658
37408930071516876158725341127622968866605210362611399728215
25679422459991243185253122720544532313520622663794272436417
87507359956181911218068991795777326796261608752343775804668
84223813614460906815885942316844499056313085691439816110468
41435976464505827310532042357277805504151076128744133166097
70400343561555943556993103725670073628460112439243800517217
17946648151586517714791609426531867375357616728998278915676
58199185014614703946969879000550578218043674277377855307968
52925731007044050355286577065656889113413367817192934796097
51349965199241672156885820419323697826495675216785846761301
66505149750837355470484537680891710657918204629663740914858
51328987371292879351434591758137218308213817683744449366969
84757491555027227218191496737306894525429493301724974763488
02878923380972880989819941626981662787664453931670154635487
31610660994478782022049824681885420029046846763098262298
89306798208587300602722354767354500448057391481009249110107
93387058874499065448114445643788142392205726681802780327985
73470136681753346929095906271088971584210825489831313413875
67612788549048657824912624883639420318879265232485613570475
73997090467104480778132423835257758424180335745170573652705
54197950691951908858510985383906254985074673094196111657807
83869871331034408636054845107081922257029648252724270305685
99507491876725741414282227189033471727764395434254185950990
74729062595276296218468117193679017860241798951200649296133
06517810763374494997293082055502432076618464586027616119817
56767737363601899914919571750573461334948379308274782665385
26109388871646107637707669952322121063841012111950272802819
21473212133919391385171174018054543600453475322352999580219
23292027677884065299422286086252105068056807793476844454707

28320229479895050738642250650424537785366800824269336818
81662317694955672636170867065177268568641882560696136399 37
89380923630615342066499106771216678307265280650651154307 87
82208618706781689410974317040601596067801396177706020483 8
32551073046418256167867786677666411458882950772884597096 43
46546857260085067375205588321834061968066477136954754650 5
82659722182787527038013350885360773847158970095196369406 6
44986845955931896822762457057294441289666846719625035790 4
35931009430361335058057283719525424750533492243401220689 1
54316788170873900888499149058827913507680455068280339445
42308221148888187376496354399413641511521268300533409275 32
30471448815684295521726253123958196789418655868201079529 18
45929630207675781253000000000000000000000000000000000000
00000000000000000000000000000000000000000000000000000000
00000000000000000000000000000000000000000000000000000000
00000000000000000000000000000000000000000000000000000000
00000000000000000000000000000000000000000000000000000000
00000000000000000000000000000000000000000000000000000000
00000000000000000000000000000000000000000000000000000000
00000000000000000000000000000000000000000000000000000000
00000000000000000000000000000000000000000000000000000000
00000000000000000000000000000000000000000000000000000000
00000000000000000000000000000000000000000000000000000000
00000000000000000000000000000000000000000000000000000000
00000000000000000000000000000000000000000000000000000000
00000000000000000000000000000000000000000000000000000000
00000000000000000000000000000000000000000000000000000000
00000000000000000000000000000000000000000000000000000000
00000000000000000000000000000000000000000000000000000000
00000000000000000000000000000000000000000000000000000000
00000000000000000000000000000000000000000000000000000000
00000000000000000000000000000000000000000000000000000000

0000000000000000000000000000000000000000000000000
0000000000000000000000000000000000000000000000000
0000000000000000000000000000000000000000000000000
0000000000000000000000000000000000000000000000000
0000000000000000000000000000000000000000000000000
0000000000000000000000000000000000000000000000000
0000000000000000000000000000000000000000000000000
0000000000000000000000000000000000000000000000000
0000000000000000000000000000000000000000000000000
0000000000000000000000000000000000000000000000000
0000000000000000000000000000000000000000000000000
0000000000000000000000000000000000000000000000000
0000000000000000000000000000000000000000000000000
0000000000000000000000000000000000000000000000000
0000000000000000000000000000000000000000000000000
0000000000000000000000000000000000000000000000000
0000000000000000000000000000000000000000000000130
8948114465174795123603548945492907251024172058822791751270 6
315775959573028069494819317749753909502 8808... 万

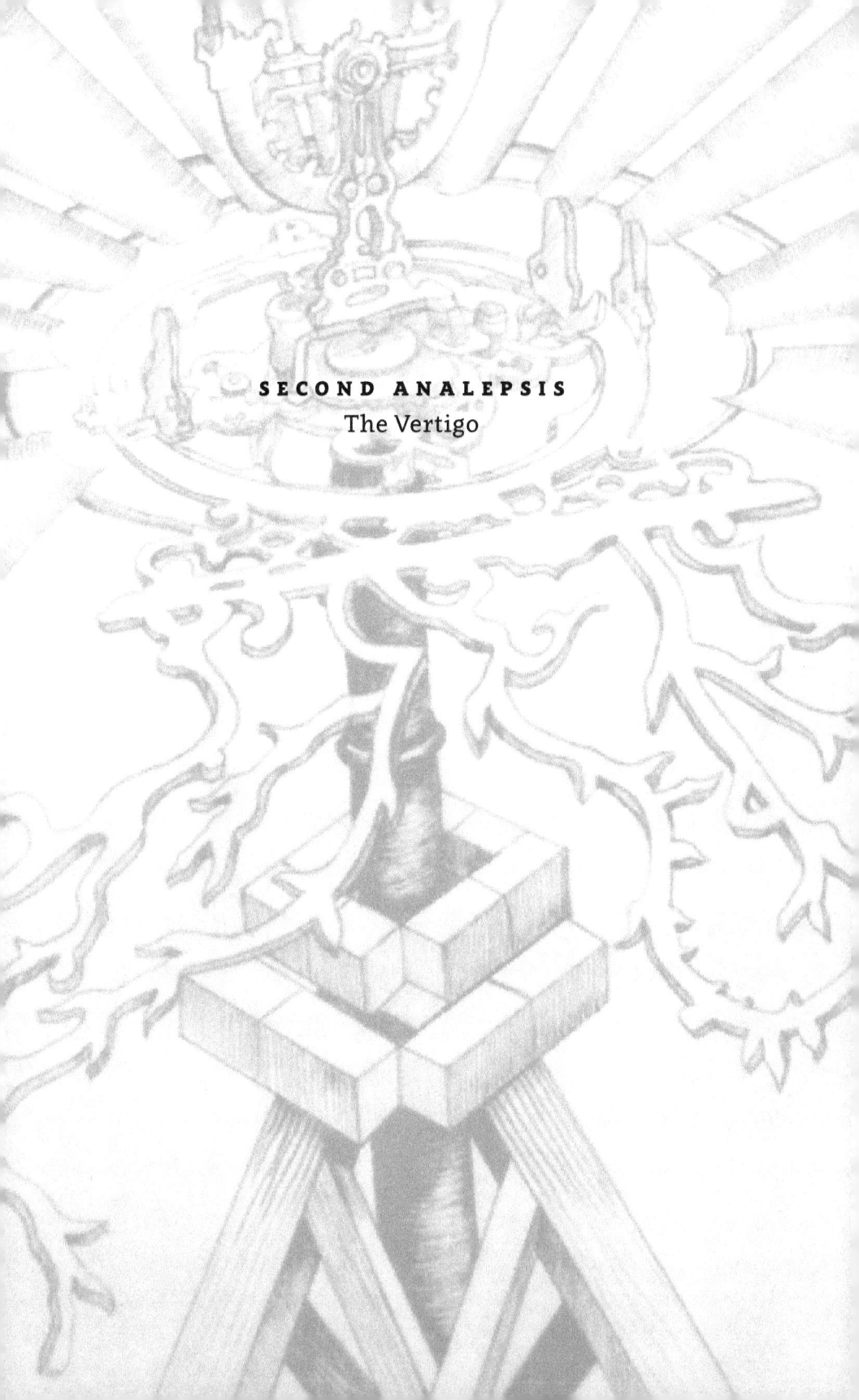

SECOND ANALEPSIS
The Vertigo

The word that remains from the beginning of the world could still be heard. He picked up a handful of sand that went slipping through his fingers. Calculus: with those fleeing atoms began and ended all cogitations on the number

MARGUERITE YOURCENAR

Policarpo walked quickly, drawn on by his body's inertia toward the house of the viceroy, which grew ever closer. When he looked up at the roof of clouds that covered the sidereal world in wickedness, he noticed the storm had died down. He was sweating copiously. The few blocks that separated him from the place where the vile machine slumbered grew distorted in his vision, they seemed to stretch between the rows of public lamps whose light hurt his eyes. Their brightness seemed to him overly intense, he had never before seen a light that gave him vertigo. The sky above threatened to fall down.

Minutes before, De Salazar had realized that a warm wetness was trickling down his left side, through his clothes, an intense scarlet thread: it was flowing blood. In his fight against the throat-cutter he had not quite managed to evade his weapon, but he could hardly feel the wound produced from their encounter's brutality. He slid on a wet cobblestone and fell to the ground. The sky expanded and contracted like the very jaws of the night, with its infinity of abysses ready to devour him. Pulling together all his hatred, he stood up to continue to his goal. At that instant, he looked up again at the haze that hid the stars. *There are not so many stars.* The length of the street was like a horizontal well, and at its bottom he could just make out the source of his fears. Nearing the viceroy's house, he breathed heavily and paused to think under the lintel of a wood and stone doorway. It would be difficult to get past the guards of the official's residence. But, determined, he made for the front of the house, willing to face anyone and to enter, even if it were the last thing he ever did. He cleared his hollow throat. He had never expected a spectacle like the one before him: just to one side of the entrance, the guards lay drunk, strewn on the steps of the shallow staircase that led to the door. They dozed, wet under the rain. Of all the police forces in New Spain, the one that ought to be most alert, safeguarding the viceroy and therefore the king and therefore the kingdom itself, was this one, the one tasked with drawing its sword even at the cost of its own life, with remaining on constant alert and in readiness for battle, the very one that De Salazar now found before him in such a pitiful state. For centuries, watchmen have fallen asleep, trusting that their instincts will awaken them before the coming of dawn puts an end to their nocturnal duties. For centuries, watchmen have drunk liquor and collapsed at their posts. Policarpo saw the keys that hung from the belt of one of the guards. With great care, he plucked them from their hook, and it is thusly that De Salazar y Hurtado entered, after midnight, the residence of the man who represented the king of Spain and, therefore, God. With his murderous hands he pushed open the door and made his way inside the sleeping house.

Inside it was dark, the shadows of unknown objects hidden in the greater shadow of the night, to which his eyes swiftly adapted, accustomed as they were to remain open over long nights, stalking victims in the darkness, long before the dawn. He made his way to the largest room, where he supposed the *Wheel* must be housed. His breathing grew labored and his side throbbed. It was not difficult to find the room; it was the most accessible of them all, and he had been there before. A rush of discouragement swept through his body when he noticed the absence of the *Wheel*: there was nothing there, the room was empty and its silence seemed to give off a heartbeat of stillness. His eyes remained fixed on the wall when the act of breathing began to provoke a stabbing pain. He raised his hand to the laceration and lifted the cloth that covered it: then he understood the gravity of the wound. The throat-cutter had landed a deep thrust in his side, but he had not noticed in the heat of the encounter and in his rush to reach the place where he now stood. His blood flowed without pause. If the machine was not there, it must be somewhere else in the house. His loathing for the beings that were sleeping in that place made his fingers tense for the practice of death: for his fingers, the viceroy and his wife were merely throats: the fattened pigs that had greedily seized the artefact, reduced to dust... Policarpo explored other hallways on the ground floor and then climbed the stone stairs toward the royal chambers. Along the way, he tripped over ostentatious furniture, carved out of precious woods from the Orient, cedar and varnished acacia. There were vases from China, little statues sculpted in Florence and Naples, stones from Cairo, and, above all, gold and more gold. The machine was not there either, not even the cloudiness of its fog. A trickle of blood dripped down in his footsteps, he felt his own heat against his wet clothes. From the wall to his right hung a lamp within which danced a weak flame. The murderer reached one of the bedrooms. Beside the door, in its little niche, he looked at the image of Saint Teresa and remembered the neck of the saint he had once gripped in his homicidal fever. With stealthy steps, he snuck into the adjacent room, where the odor of his fetid flesh mixed with the breath of the viceroy, who snored like a guttural animal in the depths of its cave. De Salazar found himself before two bulges covered in blankets of fine wool. María Antonia slept with her back turned to her disappointment of a husband, the bitter and hopeless old woman sunken into a sleep that was bought, whose price had risen. The marquis, on the other hand, lay face-up with his eyes half-open and his beard dirtied by the thick saliva that welled up from his mouth. His snorts made him seem another person entirely from the one who was seen every day in the court, nepotistic and cynical, because they revealed him in the primitive and unhealthy condition of his carnal body. Forgetting his pain, Policarpo drew closer and stared down at him for a long time. He passed his fingers over the threads of the viceregal pijamas, he softly stroked the sleeping man's beard and then, near the neck, he placed his strong and experienced right hand. Their faces were close, and his sick breath coated Branciforte's face. The pain returned with greater intensity, the palpitations pierced his being. On the floor, his blood had formed a thick puddle and the stabbing pain, now relentless, made him double over until he fell to the floor. Every object in the world spun in infinite circles. He was out of breath. Under the royal bed, Policarpo suddenly thought he saw the faces of the dead that, while alive, had twisted between his hands. They were looking at him! The knife's blow had been final. He lost all sense of direction. With painful slowness, pausing now and again to tremble, he stood up and staggered into the hallway that led to another room. He fell again and again, every time he stood up. His fury was too great, as was the quantity of air he was breathing. That knife could not be the cause of his death, not now, when he was about to undertake such an important task, to save himself from the absurd. A few steps onward, he found the threshold of another room, and he entered. There slept the young Carlota. Her breathing was soft and quite different from that of the sleeping noisemakers in the other room. She gave off an aura of peace. Beside a small shelf, with orange blossoms in a vase, stood the *Wheel*, cutting through the tenuous and delicate semi-darkness of the lamp whose light filtered through the door. De Salazar's cold, rigid gaze regained its expression before the machine. His hand covered the throbbing wound, his fingers sought to prevent his energy from escaping as it abandoned him at the end of his search. He lurched violently forward, like a drunk in the face of a cold night's breeze. The artefact was mere footsteps away. Carlota's breath, serene and sweet, interrupted his vision. When he looked at her, he experienced something strange. It was an electrical current running through his entire torso, from the pit of his stomach (the place of the most intense feelings) to the top of his throat: a sensation different from any he had experienced in his life. For the first time, Policarpo was able to feel wonder at a woman, not one like Crescencia, the prostitute of his errant wanderings, but someone sweet. It was the brief instant of an ephemeral glimmer that comes and is then lost in the deep. For the first time, he was moved by a feminine beauty, just as he reached another, different and soulless objective: the metal machine. He wanted to caress another marvellous object: the rosy cheeks of Carlota and the lock of smooth hair that lay on her pillow. The objects and the night began to blur, the things blended together and moved from their natural places and the world was inverted in a vertigo of infinity and nothingness at once. *There are not so many stars.* The faces of the dead appeared again and faded away among the bedroom's furniture, which also formed numbers of diverse orders and the ticking of distant clocks and childhood and anguish and death. Suddenly the disappearing objects throbbed into another clarity, that of a young face submerged in dreams, a face of tender lips and a slender neck that, for the first time, he looked upon and did not want to wring. It was the night of first times. For the first time, he did not listen to that tender breath in order to count each time it inhaled and exhaled. He listened to it with the unusual pleasure of hearing life, just as days before he had realized that he no longer strangled in search of a number, but rather for the simple joy of doing so. In the night of forgetting one may understand the meaning of things, but it was too late. It had always been too late for everything.

His dizziness made him turn his head and there, again before his eyes, from an immeasurable distance, was the machine. In his side, the stabbing pains were now a imperceptible tickle. The *Wheel* did not leave his gaze, and it remained fixed in his mind. The numbers became vague notions while his flesh began to accept another state, the state of the infinite into which everything dissolves. Carlota's face spun around him and then the machine. Momentarily, both were going, both coming, and they made him seasick, then both fused together, two indistinguishable beings, one from the other: the machine-woman. A distant echo rang within it: *the machine that calculates numbers*. It was his counterpart. Policarpo calculates. The machine calculates. The All-Machine. There would be no more. De Salazar was near death. A lower category of world that floated everywhere like a projection fused and grew confused with the world, it trembled, expanded, and contracted, creating disordered shadows. His mind had passed from the state of fixity to the state of the machine, the state of the Machine before him to which consciousness clung while the void began to fill everything. Policarpo fell to his knees before the Machine in an unconscious act that was solemn and obscene all at once. It was an act of adoration. Then he fell face-down and, as he lost himself to unconsciousness, he watched how the Machine faded away with him and with the world. ᚬ

To Humberto Macedo (may he rest in peace), who read the full text of my final draft and made invaluable adjustments. To my friend Jaime Mesa, for reading the very first version of the novel in 1999. To the team at Malaletra Libros, and especially to Eugenio Santangelo, for their erudition and enthusiasm in improving the text in its previous electronic version. To Javier Vargas de Luna, for the generous prologue he wrote to mark the book's republication. To the great Yuri Herrera, for generously offering his endorsement on the back cover. To Omar Villasana, who brought a bilingual version to the United States. To Arthur Dixon, for his painstaking translation to English. To Leah Duncan of Wayne State University, who carried out a theoretical study of this work, which means a great deal to me.

Pisot's number, from the *proleptic* part of the novel, is an abstract entity generated with *Mathematica*©, a program by Stephen Wolfram. This number is attributed, among others, to Charles Pisot, and it can be viewed on the *Wolfram Reference* website using the following QR code:

www.ingramcontent.com/pod-product-compliance
Lightning Source LLC
Chambersburg PA
CBHW021929170626
46807CB00007B/3041